DEATH'S

DOOR

ALSO BY BETSY BYARS

After the Goat Man
Bingo Brown, Gypsy Lover
Bingo Brown and the Language of Love
Bingo Brown's Guide to Romance
The Burning Questions of Bingo Brown
The Cartoonist
The Computer Nut
Cracker Jackson
The Cybil War
The Dark Stairs: A Herculeah Jones Mystery
Dead Letter: A Herculeah Jones Mystery
The 18th Emergency
The Glory Girl
The House of Wings
McMummy
The Midnight Fox
The Summer of the Swans
Tarot Says Beware: A Herculeah Jones Mystery
Trouble River
The TV Kid

A HERCULEAH JONES MYSTERY

DEATH'S

DOOR

BY BETSY BYARS

VIKING

VIKING
Published by the Penguin Group
Penguin Books USA Inc., 375 Hudson Street, New York,
New York 10014, U.S.A.
Penguin Books Ltd, 27 Wrights Lane, London W8 5TZ, England
Penguin Books Australia Ltd, Ringwood, Victoria, Australia
Penguin Books Canada Ltd, 10 Alcorn Avenue, Toronto, Ontario,
Canada M4V 3B2
Penguin Books (N.Z.) Ltd, 182–190 Wairau Road, Auckland 10,
New Zealand

Penguin Books Ltd, Registered Offices: Harmondsworth,
Middlesex, England

First published in 1997 by Viking,
a division of Penguin Books USA Inc.

1   3   5   7   9   10   8   6   4   2

LIBRARY OF CONGRESS CATALOGING-IN-PUBLICATION DATA
Byars, Betsy.
Death's Door / by Betsy Byars.
p.   cm.—(A Herculeah Jones mystery)
Summary: Super-sleuth Herculeah Jones's investigation of the
attempted murder of Meat's uncle leads them to a mystery
bookstore named Death's Door.
ISBN 0-670-87423-X
[1. Mystery and detective stories.]   I. Title.   II. Series:
Byars, Betsy.   Herculeah Jones mystery.
PZ7.B9836Dg   1997
[Fic]—dc20   96-34425   CIP   AC

Printed in U.S.A.
Set in Meridien

CONTENTS

Contents

DEATH'S

DOOR

1
A FACE AT THE WINDOW

Herculeah Jones sat in a window booth at the Kit Kat Cafe. She was watching the motel across the street.

She had been here for most of the morning, ever since her mom had sent her. Her mom had said, "Now keep your eyes on the Peachtree Arms Motel across the street and when a red-headed man in a tan windbreaker comes out, give me a phone call."

"But why? Who is he?"

"Just do it. It's important."

"But—"

1

"I need the information, all right? I'll explain later."

"But—"

"Five dollars an hour?"

"You got a deal."

When Herculeah first came in, she had ordered toast and orange juice. Now the toast was long gone, but she was making her orange juice last. Her mother hadn't said anything about paying her expenses.

"You through yet?" the waitress asked for the third time.

"I wish." Then Herculeah smiled and added, "I might as well be honest. I'm waiting for someone."

"He's sure taking his time."

"You're right about that." She took a tiny sip of her remaining orange juice. It was warm. Then she raised her binoculars and looked at the Peachtree Arms across the street.

"You won't need the binoculars," her mother had told her, but Herculeah had wanted them. "I might need to see something up close," she said. "Anyway, I feel better with binocs around my neck."

She adjusted the focus. She hadn't bothered with the binoculars before, but now something she saw out the window was making her curious.

Through the binoculars Herculeah noticed three things:

1) There were no cars in the motel parking lot.

2) There was a sign in the motel window that said
    CLOSED.

3) A cowboy on the sidewalk was trying to get her
    attention.

She lowered the binoculars. The face under the
cowboy hat was familiar. "Meat? Meat, is that you?"

He nodded and came quickly into the cafe. "How do
you like it?"

"The hat?"

"Yes. It's really done a lot for me. I see why cowboys
wear these things. It makes them feel manly. Want to
try it on?"

"No, thanks. I feel womanly and that's good enough
for me."

Meat sat down across from Herculeah.

"The hat really belongs to my uncle, but he's taking
a nap and won't need it. I probably shouldn't have
taken it without asking but—" He shrugged. "After I
saw how I looked I couldn't help myself."

"I'd like to meet your uncle."

"Now's your chance."

Meat peered at his reflection in the Kit Kat window.
Then, satisfied, he leaned across the table toward Herculeah. "So what are you doing in here?"

"I'm supposed to be watching the motel across the street for my mom."

"Why?"

"So I can call her when a certain man comes out, but you know what I'm beginning to think?"

"What?"

"I'm beginning to think my mom sent me over here just to get me out of the way. The motel is closed. Look at it." She offered him the binoculars, and he took a look for himself.

"Nobody's going to come out of there, Meat."

"Unless he's a workman or a watchman or something."

"If he's a workman or a watchman, where's his car?"

Meat caught a glimpse of his reflection in the metal napkin dispenser. What a hat: the tall crown, the purple band, the peacock feathers tucked inside.

"So why is my mom paying me five dollars an hour to watch it? Five dollars, and my mom does not part with money easily. So what is going on?"

The waitress came to the table holding a pad and pencil. "What can I get you?" she asked Meat.

"Nothing, I'm on a diet—oh, maybe a glass of water."

"Anyway," Meat said, turning back to Herculeah, "getting back to Uncle Neiman—"

4

"That's his name? Neiman?"

"He was named for a store."

"You gotta be kidding."

"No. All my mom's brothers and sisters were."

Herculeah looked at him in amazement. "I've heard of people being named for towns and states and even characters on soap operas, but stores?"

"My aunt Tiff was named for Tiffany's. My aunt Macy was named for—"

"I can guess that one."

"My grandfather had no idea his kids were being named for stores. He didn't have a clue. The only store he knew was Ace Hardware. But when Neiman came along and he raised a fuss, my grandmother told him it was either Neiman or Marcus. It was too late then to unname everybody."

The waitress came back to the table. "We're out of water," she said.

"Oh, come on, Meat, let's go. This is stupid. We're wasting our time." Herculeah got up and hooked the strap of her binoculars around her neck.

They paid and left the Kit Kat, and walked to the intersection. Herculeah paused at the phone booth. "What are you doing?" Meat asked.

"I've got to call my mom. She told me to call as soon as I saw the red-headed man."

"But he wasn't there."

"That's the whole point." Herculeah stepped into the phone booth, deposited a coin and dialed her mother's number. Her mother's voice said, "Mim Jones's office."

"He just came out," Herculeah said.

"Who?"

"The red-headed man in the tan windbreaker. The man you told me to watch for."

There was a silence on the other end of the line.

Herculeah was the one who broke it. "There wasn't any red-headed man, was there?"

Her mother sighed. "No."

"You just wanted me to get out of the way, didn't you?"

"Yes."

"Why?"

Her mother didn't answer.

"Because somebody was coming that you didn't want me to see, that's right, isn't it? It was some-body—"

"I've got to go. Good-bye, Herculeah."

Herculeah hung up the phone and stepped out of the booth to face Meat.

"It makes me so mad when she does that. Anytime it's something interesting, she doesn't want me in-volved."

"Maybe she's protecting you from something dangerous."

"This couldn't be dangerous. My hair hasn't started to frizzle." Herculeah's hair had a way of sensing danger. It seemed to get larger, the way an animal's fur puffs up to make its body look more threatening.

"I'm going home and I'm going to find out who my mother saw in my absence."

Herculeah and Meat started walking in the direction of home. Meat glanced sideways into various store windows to admire himself in his uncle's hat. "I'm going to have to get one of these things. What do you think?"

Herculeah's mind was on another matter. "So, what store was your mom named after?" she asked.

Meat's feet took a double step as if to get him away from having to answer.

"Quit admiring yourself and answer me. What store was your mother named after?"

"I can't tell you."

"Why not?"

"My mom doesn't want anyone to know."

"Is she ashamed of it?"

"Maybe, a little. I don't know."

"Then tell me."

Meat shook his head. "I promised."

"I'm going to get it out of you. You know that don't you?"

He nodded dumbly.

"So save us time and effort."

Meat did not answer.

"What store was your mom named for?"

Meat walked, observing his shoes as if with deep interest. "Would cowboy boots be too much?" he asked. He knew Herculeah would not be distracted and she wasn't.

"How bad can it be?" Herculeah asked thoughtfully. "K-Mart? Bi-Lo? Budget Shoes?"

"Stop it. Don't make fun of my mother."

"Pic-way? Exxon?"

"Stop! Anyway, Exxon isn't a store."

"Then tell me. That's the only way you're going to get me to stop."

Meat hesitated. "If I tell you, you have to promise you won't laugh."

"I promise."

Then Meat said one word, delivering it to his shoes rather than to the girl beside him.

"I didn't hear you."

Meat lifted his head.

"Sears," he said.

2
THE GUNMAN

The gunman moved swiftly up the staircase of the old abandoned building. He moved in a crouch, taking the steps three at a time.

He had a duffle bag over one shoulder. His rubber-soled shoes were silent.

He was a big man with powerful shoulders and arms. He moved with the sinewy ease of a large animal.

He paused on the landing. He lifted his head, as if he were sensing the air. His eyes, set back beneath his brow, were small and brown. Yet there was a reddish hue there, as if he had been caught in a bad photograph. He was known as the Bull.

He glanced down the dim hall. His eyes seemed to see through the doors. He made a decision.

Quickly, without a sound, he went up one more flight of stairs to the third floor. There he paused as if in decision. This felt right. He moved away from the stairs.

He tried one of the doors which led to a front office that would overlook the street. The door was locked.

The Bull drew a knife from his pocket. He flicked it open and slid it into the lock. The door opened with a faint click.

The Bull stepped inside.

This office was old. It had not been used in years. It had closed even before the building had been condemned a year ago.

There was still some furniture—a metal desk, old filing cabinets, their drawers pulled out and empty. A three-year-old calendar hung crookedly from the stained wall—a Christmas scene—December.

The gunman shoved the desk chair with his foot. The chair rolled across the warped wooden floor and stopped with a muted thud beneath the window. He followed and stood beside it.

He leaned against the windowsill, bracing himself

on the knuckles of his doubled fists, taking in the scene from the window. He liked what he saw. There was the house and the sidewalk in front of it. That was all he needed for a clear shot of his victim.

Satisfied, he sat down and opened his duffel bag. He took out his M16 rifle. As he readied it, he began to go over his instructions in his mind.

"How am I going to know the guy?" he had asked, holding the victim's picture under the light.

He had been in a back booth of a restaurant. He was there because he was a hired killer. The two men opposite him were there because there was someone they wanted killed.

The man pulled a newspaper picture from his pocket and shoved it across the table.

"This is no good," the Bull said, "I can't even see the guy's face. The brim of the hat hides it. I could take out the wrong guy."

He had shoved the picture back across the table in disgust. He drained his bottle of beer and signaled the waitress for another.

"You got to get me a better picture."

"You don't need a better picture. The hat's enough. He never goes anywhere without it. You'll know him by the hat. You see that hat and—" The man made a gesture as if firing a gun.

The gunman had picked up the picture again and had taken another look at the hat. He memorized it until he would know it anywhere. It was a cowboy hat with a tall crown, a dark band, and peacock feathers tucked inside the brim.

"There's only one hat in this town like that, and only one man who would wear it."

"What's this guy done—the cat in the hat?"

"He seen something he shouldn't."

"Maybe he's already told."

"At that moment he don't realize what he seen. I want him gone before he does."

The gunman's eyes had narrowed. "An innocent by-stander?"

"Something like that."

"Why don't you do it yourself?"

The man shrugged. "I'm not as lucky as I used to be. I tried a little series of accidents and none of them worked. You'll do it?"

"My pleasure," said the gunman.

When the gun was ready, he took out a radio from the duffel bag. He prepared for a long wait.

The news was on. "Investigation continues in the attempted shooting of the mayor last Thursday. Police reported . . ."

He turned up the volume.

DEATH'S DOOR

The Bull had been in place at the window for an hour when a man came out of the house he was watching. The gunman tensed and threw down his cigarette. He raised his rifle to the slightly opened window.

The man was hatless, but the gunman followed him through the upper H of the gun sight. He watched as the man paused to look furtively both ways, as he hurried across the street, and, with another look both ways, disappeared into a house.

The gunman hissed his disappointment.

There was a sign in front of the house the man had entered. The gunman telescoped it.

MIM R. JONES

PRIVATE INVESTIGATOR

A small cruel smile pulled the gunman's lips at one corner. The man was probably his target—his actions had shown how afraid he was—but the gunman didn't want to take a chance. He had been hired to kill only one man. He lit another cigarette and waited.

An hour passed. The man came out of the private investigator's house. Again he looked both ways before hurrying across the street.

"Next time wear your hat," the gunman said. "You need to protect your head."

The gunman reached for another cigarette. He lit it. His small reddish eyes glared impatiently at the empty sidewalk. He blew cigarette smoke out of both nostrils.

Anyone seeing him at that moment, even not knowing what others called him, would have had only one thought.

The Bull.

3

IN THE SHADOW OF THE GIANT PEACH

"Your mom's name is Sears?"

"Yes, but don't ever, ever let her know that I told you."

Meat reached up and felt his hat to make sure it was still there. He ran his fingers over the peacock feathers tucked inside the band.

"Sears?"

"Quit saying it please."

"You know what's really odd? That I never stopped to wonder what your mother's name was. I mean, I know every person's first name on the street—Bernie,

Bessie, Cheri—and all the time I was living across the street from a Sears!"

"Stop saying—" Meat interrupted himself. "Let's don't cut through the park, all right?"

"Why not?"

"I always feel, well, threatened in the park."

"Yes, but today you've got on that wonderful hat. I thought it made a new person out of you."

He didn't answer.

"And you're with me. You're always safe with me."

Meat said, "Huh!" Then he relented. "Oh, all right, I'll go through the park, but not by the giant peach."

In the center of the park was an enormous peach. It had been given by the Peach Growers' Association for the children to play on.

"What have you got against the peach?" Herculeah said. "I like it. I went in there one time. I used to see these little kids run in and holler, and I did it. Meat, if you go inside and yell your name—or anything you feel like yelling—it will echo a hundred times, no, a thousand."

"I know."

"You've done it?"

"Not willingly." He adjusted the hat as if to reassure himself that it was still in place and he was still feeling manly.

"Go on," she urged.

16

Meat sighed. He had already told the biggest secret of his life—his mother's name. There was no reason to hold anything else back.

"This is something I never told you. It was too humiliating, but one time—this was two years ago—I was coming through the park and some boys—Ezra Cunningham, Fox Weir, and some boy about six-foot-fifty in a Falcon sweatshirt—cornered me. The boy in the sweatshirt held my arms behind my back, and Ezra pretended he was going to hit me in the stomach, only he stopped just like one micro-millimeter short."

Meat could still feel the exact spot where the blow had almost landed. He covered it with his hand.

Herculeah waited. "And?"

"And I fainted."

"Meat!"

"I couldn't help it."

"That's the second time I know of that you've fainted in a moment of crisis. Remember the other time in Madame Rosa's, when the murderer was coming down the stairs and you were alone in the hall?"

"Yes. I never faint without a good reason," he said defensively. In Meat's opinion, fainting was the only thing that had got him out of danger.

"So, what did the boys do—run off and just leave you lying there?"

"I wish they had."

"What did they do?"

"They dragged me over to the giant peach and pulled me inside. Then they left me."

Herculeah glanced at Meat. Beneath the brim of his hat his expression was pained.

"I woke up and I didn't know where I was. All I could see was the color peach. I thought I'd gone blind. I moaned, and that moan went on—well, like you said, I know it was over a thousand times.

"Finally, finally, a mother heard me and she came over. At first she thought I was that homeless man that sleeps in there sometimes, but finally she shook my foot—my feet were sticking out—and I realized where I was. It's left me with an aversion to peaches."

"You have to learn to stick up for yourself, Meat."

"I know. I know."

"One time Billy Holland came up to me in the hall at school. He said, 'How's the weather up there, Giraffe?' I said, 'What did you call me?' He said, 'Giraffe.' He had this smile on his face like he was being so cute. I said, 'You got it wrong. Giraffes are peaceful creatures. They would never do this.'

"And, Meat, I let him have it, hard as I could." She re-created the jab in the air while Meat watched with admiration. "This happened right in front of the girls restroom and all the girls coming out had to step over him."

18

She smiled at Meat.

He said, "Why are you smiling?"

"Because we went right by the giant peach. Its shadow was so long it covered the sidewalk, and you didn't even notice."

"Maybe I'm making progress. But for some reason I still feel threatened. If you want to know the truth, I feel like something terrible is getting ready to happen to me."

He glanced over his shoulder at the giant peach. He shuddered. He wanted to be home where he was safe.

"Sears," Herculeah said as they paused at the corner. She was unaware of his feeling of fear. "Sears."

"Stop saying that. We're getting too close to my house. If my mother heard you say Sears . . ."

"She'd just think I was talking about a store."

"Not my mother. She'd know I told."

They crossed the street and turned the corner for home.

Meat wasn't musical. He could hardly remember a single tune, but now his brain came up with a song. He began to hum.

Herculeah joined in with the words.

"Can you tell me how to get, how to get to Sesame Street?"

She laughed. Meat didn't.

4
THE CAT IN THE HAT

The gunman pulled his cellular phone from his duffel bag and pulled up the antenna. He punched in a number. It was the number of the house he was watching—Meat's house.

There was no answer.

"Somebody's got to be in there," he said to himself. "I know you're in there. Come on out."

He peered through the gun sight at the windows of the house, one by one. If he saw the guy in the window—and if he had on the hat—he could take him out there.

The gunman sighed. There was no movement.

He punched in another number.

"Yeah," he said into the phone, "I'm in place. I been here over an hour."

He glanced around. I'm in an old office building. Condemned. Third Floor. Corner window. I got a perfect shot at anyone going in or out of the house. I can even see the backyard, though it wouldn't be as easy a shot."

"No cat in the hat?"

"Not yet. A guy come out about a hour ago and crossed the street—went in some private detective's house. Didn't have on any hat though."

"Bareheaded?"

"Yeah."

"Then that wasn't him. This guy never goes out without that hat."

"I remembered you saying that. That's why I didn't take him out. I had a gut feeling he was the right one, though. He had a scared look like he knew somebody was after him."

"Well, somebody is."

"Ain't it the truth." The gunman paused and then said, "I just had a thought. What if he was going over to the detective's because he just remembered what he saw?"

"It's possible."

"I can take out the detective too—for a price."

"Let's talk about that later."

"I'm always open to suggestions."

"Yeah. Give me a call when it's done."

"My pleasure."

At that moment, two people came around the corner at the end of the street. One was a girl with a lot of hair. She was laughing. The man in the hat was beside her. He wasn't laughing.

"Ah, the cat in the hat," he said with a smile of anticipation.

Then he spoke into the phone: "I got him."

He dropped the phone and threw his cigarette aside. His look sharpened as he picked up his gun and slid the barrel through the open window. He pointed his gun at the couple.

He went down on one knee in a practiced move. He braced the M16 on the windowsill. His eyes gleamed reddish in the dusty sunlight.

The target was still too far away for a shot, but he was coming closer with every step. The gunman waited tensely, his eye never leaving the gun sight.

The girl was looking at the cat in the hat, laughing, saying something that caused the man to attempt to quiet her. The cat in the hat glanced across the street.

"No, you're looking in the wrong place, pal," the gunman said. "I'm up here."

A car came around the corner and pulled up to the

curb. The Bull let out his breath in a snort of impatience. He watched as the girl bent down to speak to someone in the car. The man was momentarily blocked from the gunman's view.

"Get outta there. Get outta there," the gunman said between his teeth.

The girl glanced up and pointed as if she were giving directions.

Focused on the hat he did not notice that the girl had stopped pointing, that she had drawn back a step, that she had lifted binoculars to her face, that the binoculars were trained on him.

The car moved and once again the cat in the hat came into view.

"Right there," the gunman said. "That's perfect. Now don't move. Just keep talking to the pretty girl. It won't be so bad, pal. The last thing you'll see in this life will be a pretty girl."

He remembered the man who had hired him saying, "Take him out through the feather." He remembered saying, "I aim to please."

The gunman smiled.

His finger tightened on the trigger.

5
GUNFIRE

"Zone Three Police Department. Sergeant Mallory."

"Sergeant, this is Mim Jones."

"Hi, how're you doing?"

"Fine. Listen, I need to speak to Chico if he's not busy."

The sergeant was used to judging from people's voices when something was urgent. He said, "I'll put you right through."

"Thanks."

Mim Jones waited, twisting her finger nervously in the telephone cord.

"Mim, what's happening?" Chico Jones said.

"Chico, I hate to bother you, but I think I'm into something I can't handle."

"I didn't think there was such a thing," Chico commented.

She grimaced at his tone. "Chico, this concerns our daughter."

"Herculeah." Now both his tone and his face got serious. "Shoot," he said.

"Meat's uncle called me this morning."

"Meat's uncle. I didn't know he had one."

"Well, he does, and he's here—across the street. He asked to see me, and so I sent Herculeah off on a wild-goose chase. I knew she'd get involved. You know how she is."

"All too well."

"It turned out that the uncle is terrified. He was shaking like a leaf the whole time he was here."

"Did he give any reason?"

"Oh, yes. Someone is trying to kill him."

She paused for breath, and Chico asked, "Did he say who?"

"No. He doesn't know. A series of near-accidents have happened. A car almost ran him down. He just took that to be an accident, but then he got shoved into the path of a bus. Then a whole shelf of books fell on him—he owns a bookstore over on Fourth Street."

"And?"

"He came over here—to Meat's house—hoping to get away from it, but now he thinks it's followed him. He's convinced there's someone in the neighborhood who's going to kill him."

"And were you?"

"Convinced? Yes—no—Chico, I just don't know what to think. The man was genuinely afraid. There was no question of that. He was almost blind with fear."

"He could be paranoid."

"I don't think so."

"You think I ought to talk to him?"

"I think that's a good idea. If he really is in danger, I can't help him."

There was a pause while Chico checked his schedule. "Maybe he saw something he shouldn't or was in the wrong place at the wrong time or—"

"I suggested that but he got very insulted and said, 'Listen I'm an expert on murders and mysteries. I sell murders and mysteries. I never read a mystery I couldn't solve.'" She paused and then added, "One other thing."

"What's that?"

"I want Herculeah out of this neighborhood. I want her to spend a few days at your place."

"That wouldn't be a problem. I can pick her up at the same time I talk to him."

"It may not be easy to convince her to go. Just the fact that I sent her on a wild-goose chase this morning has aroused her interest, but I think we have to stand together on this."

"I agree."

"When can you come?"

"Right now if you think it's necessary."

"I do."

"I'm on my way."

"Maybe I'm being overprotective . . ."

"If anything, you're too much the other way."

She gave a light laugh. "Let's just say that if I were Herculeah, my hair would be frizzling." She glanced up and out the window. "Oh, there they are—Herculeah and Meat. I am so relieved. I've really been worried. I have a bad feeling about this. You can make fun of me all you want—"

"I'm not making fun. I don't have a good feeling about this either."

"I'll call her in. I'll have her packed by the time you get here. I appreciate this, Chico. I owe you one."

As she spoke she moved away from the window toward the desk to hang up the phone.

Blamblamblam

Her head jerked up. Three rapid-fire shots, fast as a three-round burst of a submachine gun. She gave a shrill cry of alarm.

"What is it, Mim? What is it?"

"A shot. Shots. Chico, I heard three shots."

"Are you sure? It could have been—"

She moved quickly to the window, the telephone clutched to her heart. She drew back the curtain and gasped at what she saw.

"Oh, no. No!"

"What is it? What's happened?"

"No, Chico, no!"

"What?"

"It's Herculeah! Meat too!"

"What about them?"

She couldn't answer.

"What about them, Mim?"

"They're down."

She dropped the phone and rushed to the door.

"What are you talking about? Down? Answer me, Mim!" Then Chico Jones said, "I'm on my way!"

But nobody heard him.

"Keep down," Herculeah hissed.

"What did you push me for?" Meat began. He attempted to lift his head, but Herculeah forced it back.

"I said, keep down!"

Meat said, "What are you doing? Have you lost your mind?"

A moment before, just after the woman's car had pulled away, Herculeah had shoved him to the sidewalk, and it had not been a mistake, Meat thought darkly, she'd done it on purpose.

He had landed hard on his face and elbows—two of his most vulnerable spots—and Herculeah had cushioned her fall by landing on him. And the one good thing he could say about his body was that it made a good cushion for a fall.

"Those were gunshots," Herculeah said.

"Yeah, right."

"I'm not kidding, Meat. Someone was shooting a rifle at us." Although there was no one to overhear the conversation, Herculeah found she was whispering.

"How do you know?"

Meat blotted his mouth on his sleeve and looked disappointed when he didn't see a bloodstain.

"While I was giving that woman directions—remember I was pointing down the street? Well, I noticed the sun reflecting on something on the third floor of the Beaker Building."

Meat's expression was still one of disbelief.

"I looked through the binocs and saw the barrel of a gun."

"Right. You're just trying to find an excuse for knocking me down."

"Meat, this is serious. Didn't you hear the gunfire?"

"I heard noises," he admitted.

"That was gunfire." She swallowed. "Meat, let's work our way back to the shrubbery, but we've got to stay down, so he can't see us."

Herculeah began to inch her way back into the shelter of the bushes. Meat followed reluctantly. They were almost concealed when Herculeah's mom came bursting through the front door.

"Mom, get back, get back," Herculeah called. "There's somebody with a gun."

"Where?"

"On the third floor of the Beaker Building."

"Are you all right, Herculeah?"

"Yes."

"Meat?"

"Yes."

"I thought you'd been shot." She broke off. "Herculeah, I'm going back inside. I've got to call your dad back. You and Meat stay where you are."

When the door had closed, Herculeah said, "But why, why would anybody shoot at us?"

"I'm still not convinced someone did."

"Then why would I throw you to the ground?"

"Because ever since I tackled you that night in Madame Rosa's, you have been planning to pay me back."

"Meat!"

"Well, it's one explanation."

"My mom thought they were shots, and my mom ought to know. Did you see how fast she came out of the house?"

Meat nodded. He put one hand to his head and realized his uncle's hat was missing. He turned his head and caught sight of it on the sidewalk.

He said, "Oh," and began to move toward it.

"What are you doing?"

"My uncle's hat."

"Leave it alone."

"I've got to get it."

"Leave it alone!"

"Uncle Neiman loves that hat. It's his good-luck hat. He'll kill me if I let anything happen to it."

"And someone else may kill you before he gets the chance."

She searched the shrubbery for a stick and handed it to him. She watched critically as he finally succeeded in hooking the stick under the hat.

He drew the stick to him, removed the hat and began to dust it off. He broke off to look at Herculeah.

She had the binoculars to her face and was peering through the shrubbery at the third floor of the old Beaker Building.

"Keep down, Herculeah. If you really think someone was shooting at us, why would you—"

"He's not there."

"Who?"

"The gunman."

"He's gone?"

"I wouldn't say he's gone. I just don't see the gun at the window. He could be at another window. He could be anywhere."

Herculeah heard a gasp of dread from Meat.

"Well, I don't mean that he's sneaking up through the bushes, or—"

"Not that."

She swirled to look at him, her long hair fanning out around her. "What?"

"That."

He held up the hat. Wordlessly he showed it to Herculeah. To emphasize the point, he put his hand into the hat and stuck a finger out through the hole.

"And you still think we weren't being shot at?" Herculeah demanded.

Meat shook his head.

"And if I hadn't pushed you to the ground, the hole would have been right there."

She jabbed one finger at his forehead.

Meat put one hand to his head and rubbed the spot as if attempting to erase it.

Then he sighed.

"What now? You ought to be grateful to be alive, Meat."

He glanced down at the hole in the hat. "I am, but Uncle Neiman's not going to like this."

"He would like it even less if your brains were oozing out of it."

"You always know how to make me feel better."

7
PROTECTIVE CUSTODY

"I don't see why I have to be punished."

Herculeah tried to get comfortable in the car. She added, "I didn't do anything wrong."

"I wasn't aware that spending an evening with your father was considered a punishment," Chico Jones answered mildly.

"I do not feel like I'm spending an evening with my father. I feel like I'm under police protection."

Herculeah and her father were on the way to her father's apartment, where she was to spend the night. She had her own room there and often spent the night, but not like this—under protective custody.

She remembered the last thing Meat had said to her. It was a wistful remark. "I wish I had a father so I could go to his apartment."

That remark made Herculeah decide to make the best of it.

"So what do you think?" She glanced at her father out of the corner of her eyes.

"About what?"

"About what happened. The situation. The shooting. The whole thing."

He didn't answer.

"It has something to do with the hat, doesn't it?"

Again her father didn't answer.

"I know it has to do with the hat. You know why? Because when I showed the hat to you and said it belonged to Meat's uncle, you and mom exchanged glances."

"Your mom and I frequently exchange glances—particularly when it's about you."

"It wasn't that kind of glance. Believe me, I know all of your glances." She paused and tried something new.

"Well, at least tell me what the police found in the Beaker Building. Dad, I have a right to know. I was the one who spotted the gun and told you which window it was fired from."

He sighed, relenting.

"They found three gun casings apparently from an

M16. They found the imprint of a bag of some kind in the dust on the floor. They found the imprint of shoes, a knee where the gunman apparently knelt to take aim. They found cigarette butts—Winstons."

"Fingerprints?"

"All over the place, though I doubt they belong to the gunman."

"Can you get fingerprints from a cigarette?"

He nodded. "These were filters and smoked close."

"You know what I think?"

He father didn't answer. The set of his mouth was grim.

"Don't you care? Aren't you even going to ask?"

"Yes," he said, sounding tired. "What do you think, Herculeah?"

"I think there was no reason for anybody to shoot at me and Meat. We haven't done anything."

Her father shot her a look.

"Well, nothing to get us killed over. So we had to have been mistaken for somebody else. I can't be mistaken for anybody else because of my hair, so it had to be Meat. It was the hat, wasn't it?"

"It was the hat."

"The gunman thought he was shooting at Neiman," she said with satisfaction.

"Neiman?"

"The uncle. Named for the store. All the children in

the family were named for stores. And guess which store Meat's mom was named for."

"I couldn't."

"I'm not supposed to tell this—I promised I wouldn't—but you're so good at keeping things."

"If you promised you wouldn't tell, Herculeah, then—"

"Sears."

Her father's lips pulled back in an unwilling smile.

"I knew that would make you smile. Oh, Dad, can I borrow your phone?"

"What for?"

"I need to call Meat."

"Herculeah—"

"I have to. I have to tell him about the hat and his uncle."

"Look, I am taking you to my apartment to get you away from what is obviously real danger."

"But what about Meat? Nobody's getting him away from danger. The last thing he said to me was he wished he could go to his father's apartment. But he doesn't even have a father." That had moved her, and it should move her father as well. "At least I have to warn him about the hat."

"Oh, all right. I wish I could have talked to"— another faint smile—"Uncle Neiman. I'll try again in the morning."

Herculeah dialed. "You didn't see him?" Herculeah asked as she dialed. Meat's mother answered, and Herculeah held up one hand to delay her father's answer.

"Hi, it's Herculeah. Can I speak to Meat?"

"Albert is in his room."

"I've got to speak to him."

"You almost got him killed this afternoon. Isn't that enough?"

"I didn't almost get him killed. It was the hat, the hat almost got him killed. That's what I have to tell him. Whoever was shooting at us thought he was your brother. Meat can't ever wear that hat again."

"I will give him the message."

"It's really important. Look, I'm not kidding about this. And tell your brother about it, too. He shouldn't wear the hat either. That hat brings out target practice in somebody."

"I can't give Neiman your message."

"But you have to. It's a matter of life or death!"

"Neiman's not here."

The phone went dead and Herculeah looked at her father. "So that's why you didn't see him. He's disappeared."

"We'll find him."

"I hope it won't be too late."

8

Herculeah stood on the school steps, her arms crossed over her books.

Usually she walked home with Meat, but that pleasure had been denied her by her parents. This morning her father had dropped her off at school. This afternoon her mother would pick her up. It was like first grade.

"Herculeah, you want to go for pizza?" a girl called.

"I can't. My mom's picking me up."

"Dentist?" a girl waiting beside Herculeah asked sympathetically.

Herculeah shook her head.

"That's where I'm going. I'm getting braces. Everyone tells me they won't look that bad, but I don't know."

Herculeah said, "No, my parents are treating me like a child."

"Don't you hate that?"

"Every time something interesting happens at my mom's, I have to go and stay with my dad."

"Nothing interesting happens at either one of my parent's houses."

Herculeah shifted her weight and searched the line of snarled traffic for her mother's car. There was always a mad rush to get away from school. Horns blew, tires squealed.

"I can't believe my mom's not on time," Herculeah said. "I can't believe she'd let me stand out here, unprotected for"—she checked her watch—"three whole minutes."

Suddenly Herculeah caught sight of Meat's mother as she pushed through the double doors of the school.

"There's Meat's mom. I recognize the coat. She's probably here to pick up Meat. Oh, I've got to stop her. Meat's gone to the library."

Meat had told her at lunch that he was planning to go to the library and look through newspapers.

"What for?" she had asked.

"Uncle Neiman's been mixed up in something. I might be able to find out what."

"Meat, you don't have anything to go on."

"It had to be something that happened close to his shop. Uncle Neiman never goes far away from that."

"Shop?"

"The bookstore. I told you about that. Do you think you could get your dad to go through the computer files on recent crimes?"

"I'll try."

"Maybe I won't find anything, but at least I'll be safe in the library."

"Meat, call me if you do find something. I'll be at my dad's. You have the number. And I'll call you if I manage to worm anything out of him."

Herculeah turned quickly to face the girl.

"Listen, will you do me a favor?"

"Like what?"

"If my mom comes by—she drives an old red Ford, only for some reason on her car it's misspelled. It says Frod. So if you see an old red Frod, tell my mom I went inside for a sec."

The girl looked doubtful. "If I'm still here."

Herculeah ran to the school doors, glanced back once for her mother's car. The traffic wasn't moving at all. No Frod in sight.

Herculeah disappeared inside the school.

The hall was almost deserted. Herculeah called, "Mrs. McMannis."

She passed the school offices, pausing to glance inside each one—that would be the logical place for Mrs. McMannis to go—but she wasn't there.

Herculeah continued down the hall.

She saw the school counselor going into her office. "Miss Marshall, did you see a woman in a red coat? I need to give her a message. It's real important."

"I passed her in the hall." Miss Marshall pointed the way. "You can probably catch her."

"Thanks."

Herculeah ran quickly and turned the corner. At the end of the hall was Meat's mother. She was almost at the stairway. Herculeah was glad she had caught her. She ran forward.

"Mrs. McMannis! Wait up! Mrs. McMannis."

The woman stopped, but she did not turn.

"Mrs. McMannis, Meat's gone to the library. He got out of study hall early."

Still, Meat's mother did not turn. That was strange, but perhaps she hadn't heard her.

Herculeah broke into a run, eager to get back outside before her mother came.

She was at Meat's mother's elbow now.

"Mrs. McMannis, Meat went to the library." For some reason she continued nervously, "Meat's going to look through newspapers and see if he can find out why someone's after your brother."

Herculeah hesitated, suddenly uncertain. "I guess I shouldn't have told you that. Don't be mad at him. He's just trying to help. He said he would be perfectly safe at the lib—"

She didn't finish the word. As she spoke, she glanced down and saw the shoes. She wouldn't have been surprised to see boots, pumps, even bedroom slippers.

She saw men's shoes.

At that moment Meat's mother turned.

Herculeah gasped.

It was Meat's mother's coat and Meat's mother's hat. But glaring at her from under the brim of the hat were eyes that were darkly unseeing and wild. The nose beneath them flared. A stubble of whiskers darkened the cheeks.

"Uncle Neiman."

His lips pulled back in a nervous smile. A muscle twitched beneath one eye.

"I was looking for Albert," he said.

"He's—he's gone to the library," she stuttered. An uneasiness crept over her. The empty hallway, the way Uncle Neiman's hands twitched at the end of his long arms added to the feeling.

"Albert's not here?"

"No—no. The library."

Uncle Neiman peered down at her. "Who are you? Do I know you?"

"I'm Herculeah. Herculeah Jones."

His look sharpened. "From across the street? Your mother's the detective?"

"Yes."

He smiled again, and there was something sinister and crafty and not at all funny in this smile.

"Then you're even better," he said.

9

THE GIRL WHO WASN'T THERE

"Chico, Herculeah wasn't there!"

"What? When?" Herculeah's father fired the questions into the telephone.

"At school. Remember I was supposed to pick Herculeah up after school. She wasn't there."

"Mim, I'm having a hard time believing this."

"Well, believe it. She wasn't there."

"The last thing I said to her before she got out of the car was, 'Be here.' She didn't even protest. I was concerned enough to hammer it home. I said, 'I don't want any mix-up. Your mother will pick you up here.'

"She said, 'I know. I know. You've told me ten times.' I said, 'Now, it's eleven. Here.'"

"I spoke to her, too. This isn't like Herculeah. Chico, I'm worried."

"What happened?"

"I pulled up in front of the school. I was a few minutes late—four, five at the most. The traffic was terrible, Chico, every kid in the school who can drive and every kid who can't was trying to get away from the school as fast as possible.

"Finally, finally I pulled up in front of the school and she wasn't there. I was getting ready to get out of the car and go inside when one of her friends ran down the steps, stuck her head in the car and said, 'Are you Herculeah's mom?' I said I was. She said, 'I knew you must be because you're in a Frod.' She said, 'Herculeah had to run inside to give someone a message. She'll be right back.'

"Then the girl got into a car with her mother and they drove off. I waited and waited. Finally I got out and went inside the school."

"And? Get on with it, Mim."

"The school was deserted. I found the janitor—he had an armload of books—and I stopped him and described Herculeah and asked if he'd seen her.

"He said, 'I haven't seen her, but right here's her books.' And he held them out. 'There's her name.' He opened up the notebook and, Chico, they were her books."

"Where did he find them?"

"That was my next question. I was screaming at him at this point. 'Where did you find these?'

"'Back yonder.'

"'Where, exactly, is back yonder?'

"'By the steps, next to the side entrance of the school.'" Mim Jones's voice broke. "Something terrible's happened to her, Chico, I know it."

"How about this girl that gave you the message? Did you get her name."

"No, but by a miracle, a miracle, I noticed the license number on the car. See, I am good for something even if it's only remembering license numbers."

"Give it to me and I'll—"

"I already had it traced. I have some resources, you know. The car's registered to a Roberta Warrington. Her daughter's name is Betty. I'm trying to get them now, but they haven't gotten home yet."

"Keep trying. I'm on my way."

Mim Jones redialed the Warrington number. This time a woman answered. "Is Betty Warrington there?"

"Who's calling?"

"Is this Mrs. Warrington?"

"Yes."

"I'm Mim Jones. My daughter goes to the same

school as Betty. My daughter gave your daughter a message for me this afternoon, and I need to know exactly what it was."

"I'll see if Betty can come to the phone. She got braces this afternoon and she's been crying ever since she got home and saw herself in the mirror."

Mim Jones waited, twisting her finger nervously in the telephone cord.

A tearful voice said, "Hello."

"Betty! Thanks for coming to the phone. I'm Herculeah Jones's mother. You gave me a message from her this afternoon."

"Yes."

"What exactly was the message?"

"Just what I said. Herculeah saw a woman going in the school and she went after her. She said if I saw you—you'd be driving a Frod—to tell you she'd be right back."

"Did she say who she saw?"

"I don't remember."

"Try. It's very important."

"It was somebody's mom."

"Try, please."

"She had on a red coat."

"Did Herculeah say her name?"

"I can't think. My teeth are killing me. Oh, yeah, it was Meat's mom. She said Meat had gone to the library and she had to tell his mom. That's all I remember. Can I go now? I keep looking in the mirror to see if my braces are as bad as I think they are, and they're worse! Betty Jo's braces are cute, but mine are ugly!"

"Was Herculeah—"

The phone was hung up before Mim Jones could finish. She dialed Meat's number and walked to the window to look at the house, as if that would make the phone be picked up more quickly.

"Hello." It was Meat's mother.

"I'm so glad you're home. This is Mim Jones across the street."

"Oh." Mrs. McMannis did not sound pleased.

"I understand that you were at the school today, Mrs. McMannis, that Herculeah saw you and followed you inside to give you a message."

"I don't know where you got that idea."

"From a girl who was standing with Herculeah."

"I don't know what you're talking about."

"The girl said—"

"I don't care what she said. The girl's wrong. I haven't been out of the house all day."

10

Uncle Neiman grabbed Herculeah by the upper arm. He spun her around to face the door. The suddenness of the movement made her drop her books.

"What are you doing? Let me—" She didn't get to finish.

Uncle Neiman propelled her through the side doors of the school. They went down the steps so fast her feet barely touched the concrete.

"Stop! Stop!"

She looked around desperately for someone to help her. Usually the playing fields had at least a few students—someone kicking punts or scoring touchdowns.

And there was always someone on the oval track. But today the school grounds were empty. Everyone was in front of the school, starting for home.

"Let me go! I mean it!"

Herculeah struggled hard. She tried to wrench her arm free, pulling with all her might, but Uncle Neiman's grip was stronger.

"What are you doing? Listen to me. Let! Me! Go!" She jerked with all her considerable strength, but he managed to hold fast. Her head was twisted toward him and she could see the strained cords in his neck.

"This is kidnapping!"

He didn't answer. There was only the sound of his disturbed, uneven breathing. She recognized from the terrible tightness of his grip and his unnatural strength that he was a desperate man.

"Help, somebody! Hel—"

His arm went around her neck then, cutting off her cry. Her throat was caught in the crook of his elbow. She could not speak. She could hardly breathe.

She gave a strangled cry, a plea for air. His grip eased enough for her to speak.

She said, "Don't hold me like that, all right? You almost choked me. I'm coming with you. I promise. I'm coming! Look!" She took a few steps forward.

He lessened his grip on her throat but not on her arm. It was as if her arm was caught in a steel vise. She

51

wondered if the blood were cut off, as the breath had been cut off from her lungs.

"Where are you taking me? At least tell me where we're going."

They moved through the school grounds and into a side street. That street, too, was deserted except for a dark car parked halfway down the block. One of the front wheels of the car was up on the curb, as if the car had been parked by an amateur.

Herculeah didn't dare to hope there would be someone in the car, but still she began to make plans. As they passed the car, she would shove her shoulder into Uncle Neiman's chest, knocking him against the car.

That might cause him to let go, and if he didn't, she would give him a kick and—and whatever else she could manage.

They were approaching the dark car. Herculeah readied herself for attack, but she moved along without resistance now, wanting Uncle Neiman to believe she had given up her struggle.

In a few more feet, they would be there.

She drew in a breath of determination.

They were at the car now. She made herself stumble, beginning her shove—

But Uncle Neiman had a move of his own.

He released her neck and opened the door with his free hand. He thrust the front seat forward. And in the same quick gesture, he shoved Herculeah into the back seat so hard that she fell sideways and struck her head on the far window.

For a moment Herculeah was dazed. Spots swam in front of her eyes.

She straightened slowly, cradling her head with one hand.

Her mother had once told her that men of little strength, awkward men in everyday life, could become as strong and skilled as athletes when their lives were threatened.

Herculeah thought that was what had happened to Uncle Neiman.

Her vision cleared, and she saw that Uncle Neiman was in the front seat, facing forward, his shoulders slumped beneath the red coat.

She noticed three things:

1)   Uncle Neiman blocked the way out.
2)   Both car doors were locked.
3)   She was trapped.

11

Meat was in the periodical room of the library. It was the first time he had ever been here without Herculeah, and he missed her.

He glanced across the room at the microfilm machine. He had sat there with Herculeah, shoulders touching as they looked through microfilm. Today he sat alone, turning through last week's newspapers.

There had been a lot of crime: a robbery at a 7-Eleven, a shooting at a night club called Chi-Booms, a sniper who shot at the mayor—but none of it seemed to be connected to Uncle Neiman.

Meat finished and sat staring down at the stack of newspapers. He felt he had missed something. Whatever it was, Herculeah wouldn't have overlooked it.

Again he glanced at the microfilm machine. He remembered the wonderful moment when he and Herculeah had been going over the news story about the Moloch, and he had been the one to discover the Moloch's face in the picture. He had pointed it out to her!

A sudden thought caused him to flip quickly back through the papers. Where was it? Where was it? He spread the paper flat. There it was! There it was!

He got quickly to his feet. "Can I borrow a dime?" he asked the room. "Will someone please lend me a dime? I've got to copy this and I was real hungry at lunch and spent all my—"

Across the room a woman was reaching for her purse, but the gentleman sharing Meat's table already had one out. "Thank you, thank you." Meat ran for the copy machine, leaving a trail of discarded newspaper behind him.

"I'll handle it, Mim. You are far too upset."

"Yes, I'm upset. My daughter's missing."

"Mine, too."

"The woman's lying, Chico. She was at the school."

Chico and Mim Jones were standing at the front

window, looking across the street to Meat's house. Without taking his eyes from the house, Chico spoke.

"Why do you think that?"

"Herculeah told Betty Warrington she saw Meat's mother going into the school. She had on that awful red coat. Herculeah followed her inside. And now Meat's mother claims she hasn't been out of the house all day. What a liar."

"Why would she lie?"

"Because that's the kind of person she is—spiteful. Plus, she has never liked Herculeah, Chico. She claims she gets Meat into trouble."

"Well, it's the other way around this time, isn't it?" Chico Jones moved toward the front door.

"I'm coming with you."

He put one hand on her shoulder. "I need you to stay by the phone. Herculeah may call, and it's important for her to get her mother, not the answering machine."

"Chico, I'm afraid we're dealing with a cold-blooded killer."

"That's why I've got every policeman in the city looking for her."

Mim Jones reached out and covered his hand with hers and they entwined fingers as they had done in the old days.

"I'll come back and tell you what's up."

Reluctantly, Mim Jones stayed at the window, watching Chico as he looked up and down the street. He did not look like a police detective but like a man who had lost his way.

She watched as he climbed the stairs to Meat's house and rang the bell. She saw Meat's mother peer out the side window, watched her crack open the door.

"Oh, you're back."

"Yes."

"Neiman's still not here."

"Actually, it's you I wanted to speak with."

When she did not open the door the rest of the way, he brought out his police ID. She peered at it, then at his face to make sure the ID was correct, even though she had known him for years.

"I guess you can come in." She glanced at the street. "Although a person can't be too careful with all that's going on."

"I agree."

He followed her into the living room and stood at the window. "My wife spoke to you earlier. Apparently there's a conflict between what Herculeah saw and—"

"There's no conflict. I haven't been out of the house all day."

"Herculeah told a friend—a girl named Betty Warrington—that she saw you going into the school and that she followed you inside."

"Your daughter was mistaken."

"She recognized your red coat."

"Maybe she saw someone with a coat like mine. There are coats like mine all over the city. That was a very popular coat," she conceded.

"That may well be."

Her look sharpened. "What's that supposed to mean?" she asked.

At that moment, Meat flung open the front door and burst into the living room. "Mom, I've got to call Herculeah. I know! I know!"

He saw Lieutenant Jones, and his voice started down the scale.

"You know where Herculeah is?" Chico Jones asked.

"Isn't she at your apartment?"

Meat didn't like the way Herculeah's father was looking at him—as if he were a suspect.

He glanced from the lieutenant to his mother. "Has something happened?"

The lieutenant spoke. "Herculeah didn't meet her mother after school."

"She was going to," Meat said quickly. "I asked her to go the library and she said she couldn't. Her mom was picking her up."

"Herculeah was waiting out in front, and she saw

your mother going in the school, and she went inside
to give her a message."

Meat turned to his mother. "You came to school?"

"No! I have not been out of the house all day. That
maniac may still be out there."

"Would you mind checking to see if your coat's still
in the closet, Mrs. McMannis."

"Where else would it be?"

"If you don't mind checking."

"I'll look," Meat offered.

He went into the hall and opened the closet door.
His mother and Chico Jones waited. There was the
sound of coat hangers being moved along the bar, the
sound of jackets and coats shoved aside.

"It's not here, Mom," he called.

"It's got to be."

Meat's mother joined him at the closet and went
through the same search. Chico Jones, his expression
grim, watched from the living-room door.

"And your red rain hat's gone too," Meat said,
pointing to a vacant spot on the shelf.

"My hat . . ."

The truth dawned on Meat's mother slowly. An in-
take of breath was the only sign she understood. Without turning to face Chico Jones she said, "My brother
is a kind and gentle soul. He has never hurt anyone in
his life."

Chico Jones did not comment.

"If for some reason Neiman took my hat and coat and went to the school, he did not do so to harm anyone. I firmly believe that. My brother is a gentle, gentle man."

"Any man can become dangerous when threatened." Chico Jones took out a pad and a pencil. "What kind of car does your brother drive—make and model, please."

"Oh, Neiman doesn't drive."

Lieutenant Jones looked up at her, his pencil still poised over the paper.

"He can't. He's blind as a bat."

12

BACKSEAT DRIVER

"I probably shouldn't have done that," Uncle Neiman said. He mumbled the words as if he were talking to himself.

This was the first time Uncle Neiman had spoken since he and Herculeah had left the school. And Herculeah had not spoken since she had recovered from the hit on the head. She didn't intend to either.

It was as if Uncle Neiman's whole goal had been to get her inside this car. And with that accomplished, he was out of ideas.

Herculeah's head still hurt, and so did her throat.

But she had put the pain out of her mind.

Her arms were folded over her chest in a pose of defiance. Her teeth were clamped together. She was tense with anger and rage. There were many things she wanted to say, intended to say, but she would outlast him, force him to speak first.

Herculeah had passed the long moments judging her chances. She could shove Uncle Neiman's seat forward, perhaps causing his head to strike the dashboard, but how would she get out of the car?

He was too big for her to squeeze around.

She could slip over and hit the horn, maybe even yell her head off at the same time.

There was nobody to hear her.

Herculeah had quietly rolled down her window so that she could call for help if anyone appeared. But that was a just-in-case thing. On a side street like this, she couldn't count on many pedestrians.

While Herculeah was sitting there with the cool afternoon air blowing on her face, doing nothing to cool her rage, Uncle Neiman spoke again. Since he was facing forward and speaking to himself, she didn't hear his exact words.

"Did you say something?" she asked, her voice cold. To gain control, she was imagining herself an important person with a driver.

He turned his head and said over his shoulder, "I shouldn't have done it."

"Of course you shouldn't have done it! It's kidnapping," Herculeah said. "You can go to prison for kidnapping." She took pleasure in repeating the word.

"It wasn't kidnapping." He made a gesture that included most of the car. "Kidnapping doesn't have anything to do with this."

"Except that's what it is."

He was silent for a moment, apparently too upset to speak. He slumped forward. Herculeah thought he was going to cry. She didn't have to harden her heart against his tears. Her heart was as hard as it got.

"You won't get away with it. My dad is a police detective and my mom's a private eye." All the things she had wanted to say before now came out, giving her a sense of satisfaction.

She was in control! Backseat driver!

"I know," he said. Uncle Neiman almost sounded morose now. "I talked to your mother yesterday morning."

"Yesterday? So that was why she sent me to look for the red-headed man—" Herculeah broke off.

"Your mother couldn't help me though," Uncle Neiman went on as if she had not spoken. "But when I heard your name, well, my nephew Albert is always talking about Herculeah. Herculeah did this, Herculeah did that. He's bragged about all the mysteries you've solved until I know them as well as you do. And, well, you just seemed like my last hope."

Herculeah glanced at the back of his head. Her eyes focused as intently as if she were looking directly into his brain.

She took in his short neck protruding from his sister's raincoat. She saw his wide ears—Meat's ears—under the brim of his hat. He lifted one hand, and she saw his knobby wrists protruding from the cuffs.

"Help you with what?" Herculeah asked, curious in spite of herself.

"Someone's trying to kill me."

"Well, that's obvious, and they almost did kill Meat! And Meat's my best friend!"

"I know, I know."

"So who's doing it?"

Herculeah leaned forward. Gaze level, her gray eyes watched the back of his head. She didn't want to miss a word of this.

He shook his head. "That's just it. I don't know. And don't tell me I must know. That's what your mother said. I do not know."

He gave a helpless shrug, and then threw back his head in such despair that the red hat dropped into the floor of the back seat. He covered his bare head with both hands.

"Oh—Oh."

"Oh, I'll get it," Herculeah said.

She reached down and retrieved the hat from the floor of the car. She hesitated a moment and then put the hat back on his head.

"Thank you."

He adjusted the hat, pulling it lower over his face. Then he turned and peered at her from beneath the brim. "I need you to do something for me."

"I'm not doing anything for you—not one single thing."

"There's no one else."

"I'm not going to help a criminal."

"I'm not a criminal."

"You're a kidnapper. That's criminal."

"It's not kidnapping. I just need you to do something for me. I'm going to let you go. You know that. I drove to the school to get Meat, but he wasn't there. He'd gone to the library. And I can't go to the library. I don't even know which library. And look at me!"

He gave a gesture of despair at his clothing. "And I can't be out on the street. That man could be any-where."

Herculeah didn't speak for a moment. Neither did

Uncle Neiman. The silence seemed to fill the car, along with the fear. Herculeah was surprised that her hair hadn't frizzled.

"I'm not saying I'm going to do it," she said finally, "but what do you have in mind?"

"I need you to get some money."

"Rob a bank?"

"No, my bookshop's not far from here, and I always keep money in the safe."

"So you actually think I'm going to go into the store, open the safe, and bring you some money?"

"I'm hoping that's what you'll do. The shop's probably being watched, so I can't go in, but I'll give you the key. You can go in the back door. The safe's behind the fourth bookcase."

"What kind of shop is this?"

"A bookstore."

Herculeah felt a lessening of her tension. A bookstore. There couldn't be any danger in a bookstore. It was her favorite kind of store in the world—next to Hidden Treasures, the antique store.

And maybe, her thoughts raced, in the bookstore, there would be a telephone! She could call her mother! Tell her what had happened! Say, Come get me!

Uncle Neiman interrupted her thoughts. "Maybe you've heard of my bookstore. Maybe Meat's mentioned it."

"He mentioned it. It's mysteries mostly, isn't it?" She looked at the back of his head, waiting.

"It's only mystery books."

"I like mysteries. What's the name of your shop?"

Uncle Neiman sighed.

"Death's Door," he said.

13

LITTLE SHOP OF HORRORS

"Death's Door," she repeated.

It made her remember that old phrase "at death's door." People used to use it when someone was about to die.

Herculeah's hair began to frizzle. She was suddenly cold.

She glanced at her window. She thought about rolling it up, but there was still a chance she might yell for help. Also, she knew the chill was not from the outside air.

"That's an awful name for a shop."

He glanced around in surprise. "Customers like it. They chose it. I had a contest. It was between Murder for Sale, Little Shop of Horrors, or Death's Door."

"The customers didn't have much to choose from, did they?"

"Everybody who bought a book got to cast a vote. Two books—two votes. Death's Door won by a landslide."

There was a silence.

Uncle Neiman cleared his throat. "Will you at least let me drive you past?" he asked in a pleading way.

There didn't seem to be any harm in that, Herculeah thought. And besides, it would get them off this deserted street and around people.

"I'm not saying I'll help," she said cautiously.

"I know. I know."

"I'm just saying I'm willing to drive past."

"Thank you. That's all I ask."

He peered over his shoulder. "Now?"

"Yes, let's get this over with," she said. It wasn't as much fun to be in control as she had thought. Besides, now that she wasn't as afraid anymore, she was beginning to feel hungry. "I want to get home. My mother's bound to be worried. By now my father's in on it too. He's probably got the whole police force looking for me."

Uncle Neiman glanced nervously over his shoulder at the thought of the whole police force after him.

"And when I do get home—if I ever do—I won't be

able to study because you made me drop all my books. They're at school! Maybe I could just run back in the school and get them."

Uncle Neiman didn't bother to answer. He shifted clumsily over into the driver's seat. Apparently he wasn't used to women's raincoats. When he was settled at last, he reached into his raincoat pocket. He pulled out a key and fumbled trying to find the ignition.

"Is this your car?" Herculeah asked suspiciously.

Uncle Neiman didn't answer. He accidentally hit the wrong control and water sprayed onto the windshield.

"Because you sure aren't familiar with it. Maybe I ought to drive. At least I know the difference between the windshield wiper and the ignition."

Uncle Neiman didn't answer. There was more fumbling at the controls.

She leaned back in her seat and glanced up at the ceiling. "And you say you're not a criminal." She listed his offenses, counting them off on her fingers. "Kidnapping! Car theft!" She wished she had enough offenses for the other three fingers. "What do you think a criminal is?"

Herculeah could see his face reflected in the rearview mirrors. Beneath the brim of his sister's rain hat, his unshaven face was grim.

"A murderer," he said.

This time the car started.

14

Meat stood at the front window. He had been there ever since Lieutenant Jones had left. He wanted to go over and wait with Mrs. Jones, but he was aware that he, the nephew of the kidnapper, would be the last person the family would want to see.

He sensed that his mother had come into the room—he smelled cooking grease. He thought she probably sprayed herself with it, the way other women spray themselves with cologne to make themselves appealing.

He said, "Herculeah hasn't come home yet."

"Well, it's early."

"It's not," he said. He looked at his watch. "It's six o'clock."

"That late?"

"Yes." He paused. His voice grew even harder. "Your brother kidnapped her."

"We don't know that for sure," his mother said, but she didn't sound convinced.

"I do."

"Neiman's no kidnapper. He was always the best one of the children. Mama said he was the only one that didn't give her any trouble. 'Why can't you be more like Neiman?' she was always asking us."

"It's just as well you couldn't."

"There wasn't a mean bone in his body."

Meat's voice was cold. "I just hope they're still alive."

"Don't say such things. Of course they're alive. Come on in the kitchen, Albert. I fixed pork chops— the way you like them."

There was no way Meat didn't like pork chops except still attached to the pig, but for once he wasn't hungry.

"Can you imagine how this makes me feel?" he asked coldly. "To have Herculeah kidnapped by my uncle?"

Meat's mother stood in silence for a moment. She dried her hands anxiously on her apron.

To divert him, she said, "Oh, Albert, when you came in, you were very excited about something."

"Finding out Uncle Neiman had kidnapped my best friend—my only friend, might I add—put the whole thing out of my mind."

"What was it?"

"Well, it was nothing that would help us find Herculeah."

"Tell me." She was still drying her hands. "I'm as worried about Herculeah and Neiman as you are—maybe even more so."

Meat sighed. "I found a picture of Uncle Neiman in the newspaper."

"Morning or afternoon paper?"

"Afternoon."

"I can't believe it. We take that. I missed a picture of my own brother."

"Mom, he was in a crowd of people. I would have missed him too except he stood out because of his hat. That hat!" He shook his head. "I'll never forget that hat in a million years."

"I won't either. I started to throw it in the trash can and then I thought, why, what if the trash collector took a liking to it—you did—and wore it around town and . . ." She couldn't finish.

"Pow . . . pow!" Meat finished it for her.

Meat's mother went on quickly, "Go on about what you saw."

"Do you remember about a week ago when they had the parade to raise money for Habitat?"

"And during the parade somebody shot at the mayor."

"Yes."

"Nobody's safe anymore." She paused to remember. "And didn't it have something to do with drugs? The mayor's trying to clean up the city and the drug dealers don't like it?"

"Well, the paper didn't actually say that. What it did say was that it was a professional job, and if the mayor hadn't had on a bulletproof vest, he'd be dead."

"And what was Neiman doing?"

"Nothing. Standing on the corner, waiting for the parade to get by so he could cross the street, I imagine. There was a reporter on the other side of the street, and just as the mayor's car went past Uncle Neiman, there were some shots, and the reporter snapped the picture."

"I hope I didn't throw that paper out," Meat's mother said. She started into the kitchen.

"Oh, wait. I made a copy of it. What'd I do with it?" He found it on the floor of the hall, by the coat closet.

As she looked at it, Meat peered over her shoulder. "See, Mom, everyone in the picture is looking at the mayor in horror—they thought it was another Dallas—except Uncle Neiman. He's looking up, like he sees something interesting in the building across the street."

Meat's mother drew the picture closer.

Meat continued. "And whoever saw that picture thought Uncle Neiman had seen him."

"He does appear to be seeing something."

"He does."

"But Neiman has terrible eyesight. He can't see from here to there." His mother pointed to the back door.

"Yes, Mom, but whoever's trying to kill him doesn't know that."

The drive had been silent except for Herculeah's urgent shouts of "Brakes!" or "Red light!"

The rush hour had passed, and after-supper traffic was light. Herculeah was grateful for that. She felt that if she had to yell "Brakes!" one more time she was going to throw the seat forward and jump out of the car. She'd be safer outside the car than in.

Now Uncle Neiman made a wide turn onto a street with less traffic. He was still straining forward tensely over the steering wheel, but Herculeah relaxed a little.

"Can I ask you a question?" she said.

"What street is that?" he asked. "Can you read the sign?"

"Wentworth."

"Is that the bank over there?"

"First National."

"Okay, good. I know where I am. Go ahead and ask your question."

"Well, what I'm wondering is, when was the first time you thought someone was after you?"

"Last Thursday—the day after the mayor was shot. I was crossing Conning Boulevard—or trying to—and a car almost ran me down."

"You thought it was an accident?"

"At the time, yes."

"Did you see what kind of car it was?"

"Dark."

"That doesn't help much. And you didn't see the driver?"

He shook his head.

"Or the license plate?"

"Oh, no."

"I guess that was too much to hope for. So that was Thursday."

"Yes."

As a car pulled out of a side street, Herculeah cried, "Brakes!"

He slammed on the brakes. "What's that fool doing?" he asked, "turning like that."

Herculeah fell forward. She braced her arms against the front seat and it fell forward too. At that moment she had a chance at the door handle.

She reached for it with one hand. With the other, she grabbed the buckle of her seat belt. But for some reason that she couldn't understand, she stopped.

"He had the right of way. Didn't you see the YIELD sign?"

"No."

She leaned back in her seat, surprised at herself. I'm still sitting here and not out there running along the sidewalk because I'm me. I have to know what's happening. I have to be there at the finish.

"So," she continued after a moment, "what happened on, say, Wednesday?"

"Nothing." He peered over the steering wheel. "Is this Conning?"

"Yes."

"That's where I almost got run over. Want to see?" He didn't wait for her answer. "I'll show you."

Uncle Neiman made an abrupt turn from the wrong lane. Horns blew. Brakes screeched. Herculeah tightened her seat belt.

"Have you ever driven this car before?" Herculeah asked when her heart had started up again.

"No."

"Have you ever drive *a* car before?"

"A few times."

"Well, you don't drive like it. Whose car is this anyway?"

"A friend's."

"Does he know you've got it?"

Uncle Neiman ignored the question. He came to a stop in the middle of the intersection. "This is where it happened. I was standing there."

Horns blew. Traffic stopped behind. More horns.

"I see it. Go ahead." She glanced out the back window into the furious face of a driver.

"It happened the day after the mayor got shot at. Did you read about that?"

"My mom mentioned it. Tell me while you drive."

Uncle Neiman moved cautiously through the intersection.

"I had gone for lunch over at the Bistro—I always eat there—and I came home by the same way, Conning Boulevard."

"And?"

"And I started across the street, and a car came at me—I mean, *at* me. A man grabbed me by the back of the jacket and yanked me to the sidewalk or I wouldn't be here to tell about it."

"You were lucky."

"You think so? My hat fell off my head, and he did run over that. I could show you the tire marks, if I still had it."

"That is not what I would call a lucky hat. Did you happen to see the shooting?"

"The mayor?" He shook his head. "I was there but I didn't see anything."

"Maybe you saw something that you don't know you saw—some little insignificant thing. That does happen."

"Mostly in mystery books."

Herculeah interrupted to say, "Oh, I wish I had my granny glasses."

"Glasses?"

"Little round ones. They make me fog out. The whole world becomes a blur. They help me think."

"You put on glasses so you won't be able to see?"

"Yes."

"I don't need any granny glasses for that. My eyes do a good enough job of creating a fog all by themselves."

"What do you mean?" Herculeah asked.

When he didn't answer, she leaned forward.

She said, "What are you saying?" this time stressing each word.

"I'm saying I don't see anything but fog. The truth of

the matter is that I can't see from here to the next corner."

He bumped up onto the curb and off again.

"That was the next corner," Herculeah said.

"I told you."

16
MAGOO

"It's true," Uncle Neiman continued mildly when they were back in their lane again. "I'm almost blind. My friends call me Magoo."

"How did you ever get a driver's license?"

"I don't have one."

"You don't have a driver's license?"

"I used to. My eyesight was better then. Nowadays I remember my way around. I've been traveling these streets all my life."

"Stop this car. I am not kidding. I am getting out of here."

Uncle Neiman speeded up.

"I said I want out!"

"There it is!" Uncle Neiman said.

"What?"

"My shop."

He put on the brakes and came to a stop in the intersection. Herculeah glanced behind them to see if they were going to cause another traffic jam, but there were no cars in sight.

"See, I got us here, safe and sound."

Herculeah said, "Huh!" Then she glanced down the street with interest. "Which one's yours?"

"Third on the left, between Goodwill and the adult video store."

Uncle Neiman stepped on the gas and moved quickly to the corner. Herculeah peered over her shoulder.

"Aren't you going to stop?"

Uncle Neiman steered the car around the corner into the wrong lane, narrowly missing a minibus full of old people, and back again.

"I'm not even sure I saw it," Herculeah said.

She had a vague impression of a dark brick building that had once been a house. She thought she had seen a sign on the door, but Uncle Neiman certainly hadn't given her time to read it.

"I can't turn in. The man—the gunman—might be waiting for me. A woman's raincoat and hat isn't going to fool him. Did you see anybody suspicious?"

"I didn't see anybody—period. All the stores looked closed."

"That doesn't mean there's nobody there."

"Too right."

"I'm going to stop on Hunter Street. The alley goes right through to the shop. Nobody knows about the alley but the shop owners. It just looks like a space between buildings. You can go down the alley to the back door of the shop and—"

"Hey, I didn't say I was going to do this," Herculeah interrupted.

"Well, if you decide to, that's what you can do."

Uncle Neiman parked the car beside a pawnshop that had its bars up for the night. He parked the way he had before, halfway up on the curb.

"Well, here we are," he said. "You didn't think I could do it, did you?"

"No."

"And not so much as a scratch on the car."

"It wasn't the car I was worried about," Herculeah answered.

17

THE SOUND OF SILENCE

Uncle Neiman had not turned off the ignition—maybe he was too blind to find it, Herculeah thought. More likely, he was waiting for her to make up her mind.

"Are you getting out, or not?" he asked, confirming her thought.

"I'm thinking about it," she said.

Her choices, it seemed, were both unappealing. She could take a chance on getting the money from the safe without being seen by the gunman, or take a chance on driving around some more with Magoo and living through that.

85

The motor continued its hum.

"Let's go over it one more time," Herculeah said. "Tell me exactly what you want me to do."

"You will walk down the alley to the back door. You'll find it easily because there's a sign that says DEATH'S DOOR—NO ADMITTANCE."

"Don't I wish," Herculeah said.

Uncle Neiman reached under his raincoat and into his pants pocket and brought out a ring of keys. He selected one key from the rest and offered it to her. The rest dangled below.

Herculeah made to move to take it.

"Then what?" she said.

"Then you'll find yourself in what used to be the kitchen of the house. Now it's where I keep my rental books."

"Used paperbacks?" Herculeah asked, trying to get a feel for the room she'd be in.

"I don't handle anything but used books," Uncle Neiman said. "The rental library's a mixture—paperbacks, hardbacks, magazines. Some of these books have been in and out of the shop fifty or sixty times so they're showing their age."

"All right. So I go through the kitchen—the rental library. What then?"

"You'll pass the steps that lead upstairs. My apartment's up there. I don't suppose you'd be willing to pack a few of my things while you're there."

"You suppose right."

"I could sure use my own raincoat. I'm beginning to feel like I'm three years old in my sister's cast-off clothes."

"No."

"My mother never made me wear the girl's dresses, but those old-timey coats had a lot of wear in them."

"No!"

"All right."

After a silence, Uncle Neiman continued. "If you don't want to go upstairs—"

"I don't."

"You keep on walking. Death's Door used to be a private home, and so the two rooms across the front are the old dining and living rooms. The dining room—you'll go in there first—has ten stacks of books, five here, five here."

He diagrammed it with his hands.

"Well," he corrected himself, "it usually has that many. One of the shelves fell on me—was pushed on me, if you want the truth. It was no accident."

"Probably not."

"And I never cleaned it up. The books are still on the floor."

"That's the room where the safe is?" Herculeah asked. "The dining room?"

"No. Keep to the right. You'll pass the counter with the cash register and the telephone—"

Herculeah's heart quickened at the thought of a telephone.

"And the computer. Go past that and into the living room. There are bookcases against the back wall. One of them has a glass door. It's locked. It's where I keep my valuable books. I've got an autographed Josephine Tey."

"What's that?"

He looked at her with disappointment. "Well, she's English." He decided to give her another chance. "I've got an autographed Donald E. Westlake."

She shook her head.

"Well, who have you heard of? And don't go asking for an autographed Nancy Drew, because they were written by anybody that felt like writing them. There never was a Carolyn Keene."

"I know that. Agatha Christie?" she asked.

"Not autographed." Uncle Neiman sighed. "Well, getting back to the keys—this little one opens the glass door. You take the books from the left side of the top shelf—lay them carefully on the floor, some of these books are worth hundreds of dollars—and you'll see the combination lock. I'll give you the combination. It's fourteen, left—"

"I haven't absolutely agreed to do this," she reminded him.

They sat there in silence.

"Oh, give me the keys," she said.

He turned quickly. "This one for the door, this one for the glass door. And the combination is fourteen, left, fifteen, right, then all the way around twice to seven."

Herculeah repeated the numbers.

"I could write them down for you."

"Maybe you should. I'm usually good with numbers, but I'm nervous about this."

"He's after me, not you."

"I hope you're right."

She took the slip of paper he handed her, unbuckled her seat belt and climbed out of the car. She paused on the sidewalk for a moment.

Uncle Neiman cut the motor, and a silence descended upon Herculeah.

"That way," Uncle Neiman said, jabbing a finger toward the overgrown alley.

"I know."

She started forward. They alley seemed to pull her into something unpleasant, something primeval even.

She picked her way slowly through the weeds and lit-
ter. Daylight was fading, and the alley, with buildings
on either side, was cut off from the twilight and
evening breezes. The day was darkening fast.

Suddenly Herculeah wished Meat was with her.
Meat wasn't much of a watchdog—he had even fallen
asleep on the job once at a place called Dead Oaks—
but he was a wonderful friend. Her heart wouldn't be
beating in double-time if Meat were at her side.

Painfully aware of her aloneness, she moved carefully down the alley, looking around as she went. She
heard a noise and spun around. A cat ran from behind
an overturned garbage can.

"Don't do that to me," she told the cat.

She got to the back of Death's Door before she
wanted to. The keys were moist in her clammy hand.
She put the right one in the keyhole and turned.

She felt the click as the lock opened. She pushed the
door slightly ajar.

Again Herculeah paused to look behind her. The
alley seemed deserted. There was only the yellow cat
in sight, watching her warily with slitted eyes, waiting
until she was gone and he could check the garbage
again.

She pushed the door open all the way.

Ahead of her, the dim, ghostly stacks were filled,
overflowing with old books. She breathed in the com-

90

plex odor of hundreds of books and the hundreds of people who had read them.

Herculeah took one last look at the alley. She tried to take comfort in the fact that she saw no footprints in the dry weeds but her own and that the cat had been as startled when he saw her as if she was the first person he'd seen in his life.

Herculeah stepped over the threshold. As the stacks of old books seemed to reach out for her, she had the odd feeling that she herself was not stepping forward but backward in time.

A nerve tightened at the back of her neck.

"Get it over with," she said to herself.

18
NOW THE BULL

The Bull took his cellular phone from the duffel bag. He pulled up the antenna and punched in a number.

The phone was answered with the usual one word, "Yeah?"

The gunman said, "It's me." He didn't have to say anymore. His gravelly voice was his identification.

"So, where are you?"

"I'm across the street from the cat in the hat's bookstore. I'm in an apartment building. Number two-oh-one, to be exact. It's empty"—he gave a laugh that was without mirth—"except for me and my M16."

He reached down and gave the weapon a pat, as if it were a favorite dog.

"Nobody saw you go in?"

"Nah. Hey, guess what the dude's bookstore's called. Death's Door—appropriate, huh?"

"Let's hope so. Any sign of him?"

"Not so far. A car came by driving kind of crazy ten minutes ago. I thought it might be him but he didn't stop."

"Keep watching. If the police get him before you do, it's going to very unfortunate—for all of us."

The man emphasized the word "all," turning the line into a threat.

"I'm aware of that. But this is his home, man. The dude lives over the bookstore. He's gotta come here sooner or later."

"Let's hope sooner."

"Hold on a minute. I thought I saw something moving over there."

Both men held their phones tensely. The Bull moved closer to the window and peered through the glass at the darkened bookstore.

The streetlights had just come on, casting a faint amber glow beyond the store window and into the interior of Death's Door.

"Nah, maybe it was just the streetlights, but I'm gonna keep watching."

"Do that."

"I might go over and make myself at home." Another humorless laugh. "At least I'd have something to read."

"You better stay where you are."

"Unless I see a light go on or something else moving around."

The man on the other end of the phone conversation said, "What if he gets in by some back way we don't know about? What if he gets in and calls the police."

"Calling the police is one thing you don't have to worry about."

"Yeah?"

"I took care of that. I cut the phone wires."

"Well, take care of the rest of it."

The man hung up with those words, and the gunman punched the Off button and lowered the antenna. He turned his full attention to the bookstore across the street.

His red eyes seemed to pierce the brick walls as he lit a cigarette and blew smoke out of both nostrils.

"Come on," the Bull begged.

His finger curled impatiently around the trigger of the M16.

"Come on."

19

Herculeah closed the door behind her reluctantly. She would have liked to leave it open, but if she did, anyone could follow her inside.

In the sudden darkness, her fingers moved over the lock, memorizing the mechanism, making sure she knew how to get it open fast. She practiced a few times before she turned to face the stacks of books.

It was dark in the bookstore. Some bookcases had been placed against the windows, blocking out what light was left of the day. The silence was absolute. She couldn't even hear the hum of a furnace or the traffic in the street outside. Maybe books absorbed sound.

A Herculeah Jones Mystery

Herculeah had feared that the gunman might be waiting inside the bookstore, but the unearthly silence told her he was not.

She stepped forward and a board creaked beneath her foot. Well, at least nobody will be able to sneak up on me, she thought. She was not comforted.

Herculeah felt her way along the stacks of rental books, past the staircase that led to Uncle Neiman's apartment. She could see a faint light at the top— probably from outside. She took a few more steps, moving once again into darkness.

Her leg struck the side of a chair. Herculeah cried out in pain as the chair toppled over, strewing books onto the floor.

"You didn't mention the chair," she sang to the absent Uncle Neiman. She paused to rub her shin. "Well, at least there's no point in trying to be quiet."

Skirting the fallen books, she moved to the door of what had once been the dining room. There was more light here. The streetlight through the dusty window gave the room a misty look.

Herculeah wasn't pleased that the streetlights had been turned on. Sure, she could see better, but so could anyone outside, looking in. She paused in the doorway, caught by an uneasy feeling.

She had the feeling that someone was out there, the gunman who had shot at them before. She remembered her statement, "I didn't see anybody—period," and Uncle Neiman's answer, "That doesn't mean there's nobody there."

She tried to shake off her dread. She told herself she had never had time for hesitation and foolishness.

She moved carefully to the first bookcase. She could see the scattered books on the floor by the window, the books that had fallen from the shelf someone had pushed at Uncle Neiman.

She moved carefully toward the living room. She was aware that as long as she was behind the stack, she was hidden from the street. But now she was at the end of the bookcase, and there was a two-foot space before the next one. She went down in a crouch and slipped across.

At the end of the dining room there was an entrance hall—Uncle Neiman hadn't told her about that. The door that led outside was glass.

Here, Herculeah got down on her stomach and inched across, crocodile-style. She stayed down until she was at the counter. Then she straightened.

Only a wire rack of paperbacks stood in her way. She stepped around it, brushing it so that it gave a half-turn, groaning in protest.

"Sorry," she said.

In the dim light the objects in front of her began to take shape. There was the computer . . . the cash register . . . a rack of tapes . . . and—and something unfamiliar crouching behind them.

She froze. A car passed in the street and in the glow of the headlights she made it out. A rubber plant.

And there—there was the telephone.

Herculeah smiled. It was her first real smile since Uncle Neiman had forced her from the school earlier that afternoon.

Now at last she could call her mother. Her mother would give her the usual frantic, "Herculeah, where are you?"

And she would tell the truth. "Mom, I am at Death's Door."

Her smile broadened.

She picked up the phone and held it against her chest for a moment, overcome with relief and with the thought of her mother's strength—and her father's! Her dad was bound to be in on this too. He would be as frantic as her mother, though he wouldn't show it.

And her father would act. He would have a squad car here in minutes, policemen running up to the store, guns drawn. She would tell the police about Uncle Neiman and where he was parked. She would have to.

But she would not tell them about the kidnapping. Somehow she had begun to feel affection for Uncle Neiman in that brave, blind drive across the city.

She lifted her head. She noticed that her hair was beginning to frizzle.

Why is that, she wondered, when rescue was just a phone call away. She smiled. The phone company could use something that comforting in their ads.

She picked up the phone, punched in her number and lifted the phone to her ear.

She heard no sound of a phone ringing.

She held the phone up to what light there was. Sometimes you had to click a phone. She found that button and clicked.

She heard no dial tone.

The line was dead.

And with that thought came others that were even worse.

Somebody has cut the wire.

And whoever did it is out there.

A squad car came around the corner.

Uncle Neiman's eyes weren't good enough to see that it was a police car, but he ducked out of sight anyway. He didn't want to be seen by anyone.

Also, ever since Herculeah had mentioned the fact that every policeman in the city was after them, he had realized that he could not be taken by the police. It was as Herculeah had said. That girl was no dummy. He was a criminal. He had turned himself into a criminal. He cringed at the thought.

It had happened against his will. He loved crime and

criminals on paper, but in real life he was a gentle, law-abiding man. Used to be, anyway. Not anymore.

He had stolen a car—it was a friend's car, but he'd taken it without asking, and if he had asked, his friend would have refused and insisted on driving him wherever he wanted to go.

He'd kidnapped a girl—that was far worse than car theft.

He tried to think of the number of years a kidnapper spent in prison, but despite all his knowledge of crime and mystery and murder, he didn't know that.

He lifted his head. The car had passed and was out of sight.

Uncle Neiman lifted the rain hat, wiped the sweat from his brow and quickly put it back on again.

Maybe it had been a mistake to send the girl in there. Maybe he should just have . . .

Have what? He couldn't think of one single thing. Of course, he would have had a better chance in the shop. He was used to it—and to the dark. He ran his fingers over his watch, feeling the numbers. Seven forty-five.

Shouldn't she be back by now? It couldn't take that long to open the safe.

For lack of anything constructive to do, he decided to back up the car and park directly in front of the entrance to the alley. That way he could see Herculeah when she came out. Well, he might not be able to see her, but he could still see motion, and he was fairly sure she would be in motion.

He reached for the ignition. "Where is it? Where is it? Oh, there."

In a fog of his own, he turned the key and felt a bump as the car backed slowly off the curb. He stopped at the alley.

Uncle Neiman waited. He didn't turn off the ignition this time. He had the feeling that he might have to get out of here in a hurry.

His head snapped up with a sudden unpleasant thought. He peered forward, but he was unable to distinguish one dashboard instrument from another.

Still he added one more thing to his pitiful list of hopes, a list that seemed to be growing by the minute:

1)   He hoped Herculeah would come back soon.
2)   He hoped she would have the money.
3)   He hoped he would get away.
And now:
4)   He hoped he wouldn't run out of gas.

Herculeah put the phone back in its cradle as carefully as if the phone were in working order. With a feeling of doom, she glanced around the shop.

She was torn between leaving immediately and getting the money for Uncle Neiman. She wanted to do what was most safe but she didn't know what that was. Or was anything safe?

If the gunman had cut the wires, he was outside somewhere. If she rushed out—

But he hadn't seen her come in. That meant he was out front. So maybe . . .

She had made no decision, but she found she was

moving toward the rare books. It was if she were sleepwalking and didn't have control over her actions. Her heart had begun to pound. Her throat was dry.

She felt in her pocket. The key was there. Her fingers curled around it. She drew it out. With her fingers, she found the keyhole. She got the key in on the third try. She unlocked the door.

Herculeah found she couldn't remember Uncle Neiman's instructions. Where were the books she was supposed to move? The top shelf—she remembered that much. Right or left?

She took off the books on the right. She set them on the floor. Rising, she felt the space against the wall. There was no combination lock.

Her hands had begun to tremble. She reached up and took down the books on the left. There it was. She was aware that she was moving faster than she had ever moved in her life. Everything was speeded up, as if to keep time with her racing heart.

She took a deep breath. She glanced over her shoulder, then back to the lock.

Now for the combination. At least that was etched in her mind: fourteen, left, fifteen, right, twice around to seven. There was a satisfying click that told her the safe was open.

At that moment she heard something that turned her blood cold. Ice water rushed through her veins.

There were footsteps on the porch.

There was a stealth about these footprints that told Herculeah whoever was coming to the door had no business there. Her heart was pounding in her ears now.

Again she was torn with indecision. She glanced at the door, gauging the distance. Did she have time to run past the door and get to the alley before whoever it was came in? Maybe she only had time to hide behind the counter. Or maybe she—

She had no time at all. There was a sharp, metallic click at the front door's lock—a knife, Herculeah thought—and the entrance to Death's Door swung open.

Herculeah flattened herself against the wall. She pulled back into the shadows.

She heard someone step inside. She heard the door close. It happened in a matter of seconds.

She heard the sound of something heavy being put on the floor—a suitcase maybe.

She heard a faint hissing sound, as if the man—she knew it was a man—were inhaling through his front teeth. It was a sound of satisfaction as if he found himself where he most wanted to be, about to do something he had looked forward to. Now Herculeah's heart was pounding so hard she wondered that he couldn't hear it.

He came forward a few steps and stopped. He was a big man—she could tell that from his footsteps—and yet he moved with the certainty of an animal. Herculeah could tell his position from the creaking of the floorboards. He took another step.

She knew he was standing in the entranceway now, probably looking from room to room, making a decision.

Let him go into the dining room, she pleaded, willing it to happen with all her might. Then let him go up the steps to Uncle Neiman's apartment.

She sent the message again and again. Go into the dining room. Go up the stairs.

Because, Herculeah thought with faint hope, if he went up the stairs, she would have a chance to get to the door. All she needed was a chance. She was as fast as any man—even one who moved like an animal.

But if he came in this room, she thought, and she felt unaccustomed tears sting her eyes, she would not have any chance at all.

There was a silence. The gunman didn't move, just stood there, feeling the air, listening. Herculeah held her breath. She closed her eyes. She now had to breath through her mouth.

Please go in the other room, she pleaded. Turn right. Turn right. Don't—

She didn't get to finish. She heard the gunman step

into the room where she stood against the wall. Her eyelids flew open.

Her knees had begun to tremble.

He took one step, another. He was coming closer. It was as if he were a hunter stalking a helpless creature, and even though he didn't know exactly where his prey hid, he had plenty of time to find out.

Herculeah could smell him now—cigarette smoke and sweat. In the light from the street, his right hand came into view—a hand as big as a ham. And in it was a gun, a silencer on the end.

If he comes on this side of the stacks, he'll see me, she thought. She resumed her mental pleading. Go between the stacks. Between the stacks. Between—

This time it worked.

The man stepped between the bookcases, and she could see his silhouette through the gaps in the books. He was huge—massive shoulders, arms bulging against the sleeves of his jacket. She held her breath as he made his way through the room.

He paused as if looking for a book, though Herculeah knew he was not. Perhaps he had heard her. Perhaps he was one of those people who can sense another's presence. Perhaps he had the animal ability to smell a victim's fear. There was plenty of that.

All at once she remembered something Uncle Neiman had said—something about a stack of books falling on

107

him. He had thought it was one of the attempts on his life.

So these stacks could be pushed over, if someone had the strength.

Herculeah drew in a deep silent breath. I have the strength, she told herself. I have to have it.

With that thought, she could feel it building in her like a force of nature, something that could not be held back.

The gunman was directly across from her now. She dared not move. She'd have to take two steps to get to the bookcase and that might be all the warning the man would need.

He drew air in between his teeth. There was that hissing sound, deadly as a snake's.

At that moment, the man leaned down, peered through the books, and his terrible hooded eyes looked directly at Herculeah. The eyes were red and seemed to be lit from within like something at Halloween.

"You," he said.

He exhaled and Herculeah smelled the fetid breath of death.

22

"Albert, come away from the window."

"I can't."

"Albert, that's not doing any good. You aren't help-ing Herculeah by standing at the window. Come and watch TV."

"And will that help her? My watching TV?"

His mother sighed. "I can't do anything with you when you're like this."

"Then don't try. Leave me alone."

His mother came and stood beside him. Meat stiff-ened, warning her not to pat him. She didn't. She put her hand back in her apron pocket.

"Where could he have taken her?" Meat said. "You ought to know. He's your brother."

"I have no idea. My own brother is a complete stranger to me. It's probably as well we don't watch TV. Neiman could be on the news."

"Could they have gone back to the bookstore, do you think?"

She shook her head. "That's where the trouble started. The gunman knows about the bookstore."

"Do you think I should go across the street and at least tell Mrs. Jones about it?"

"They're smart people. By now they know more about Neiman than we do."

"Well, I'm going to go over there anyway."

"Albert—"

"I'm going!"

Meat had been wanting to do this for hours, but he hadn't thought of a good enough excuse.

He ran out the front door and across the street. He took the stairs to the Jones house by twos. This was the fastest Meat had ever gone up stairs in his life.

Mrs. Jones must have seen him coming, because she opened the door before he had a chance to ring the bell.

"You've heard something?"

Her face, pale with concern, lit up with quick hope. She put one hand over her heart.

Meat shook his head and watched her hope die. He wished he hadn't come.

"No, no, Mrs. Jones. I'm sorry. I wish I had heard something."

"Where are they? Where are they?"

"That's what mom and I were talking about. That's why I came over. Uncle Neiman has a bookstore, but Mom doesn't think they went back there."

"Chico knows about that. He has a squad car driving past regularly, but there hasn't been any sign of them. Where could they be, Meat? What kind of man is your uncle?"

"He was just a nice man who brought me books," Meat said. "Always Hardy Boys."

He remembered that those books always made him wish someone would write a series about the Unhardy Boys. He had considered writing the books himself, but he had never got any further than naming them Meat and Pete.

He shook off the thought. Mrs. Jones wouldn't be interested in his mystery series when her only child was missing.

He said carefully, "I guess Uncle Neiman's a desperate man." She waited, knowing there was more. "I think he went to the school to get me to help him get out of town. I wasn't there so he took Herculeah. My guess is that's what she's doing—helping him get away."

111

"Neither of them can drive—he because of his eyes and Herculeah—well, she's driven from here to the corner a time or two, but she's certainly not capable of driving in traffic."

"Have they checked the bus stations? The train stations?"

"Yes. And every policeman in the city has his picture—your mother found it for us—a description of what he was wearing and a picture of Herculeah and what she's wearing. As soon as there's any news, Chico's going to call me. I've got to stay by the phone."

"Will you let me know?"

"Yes."

She closed the door in his face, and he remained on the steps for a moment, unwilling to give up this small contact with his friend.

He heard Mrs. Jones sag against the front door, as if she didn't have the strength to get back to the phone. She asked again, "Where can they be?"

23

Herculeah ducked down. She could no longer see those terrible eyes, but it was as if their viciousness was burned into her brain.

She knew that he was waiting for her to move. If she went right, he would too. Left, and he would be waiting at that end of the bookcase.

Well, she thought, her move might surprise him. She stepped forward with a cry of fright and power worthy of a samurai. Arms outstretched, head down, she took one more step and pushed with all her strength.

The bookcase resisted. It was heavier than Herculeah had thought. For one split second, it didn't move at all, and then it rocked slightly forward and back. A few books tumbled to the floor. Then Herculeah put her shoulder to it, and with a groan, it toppled. There was an oath of surprise from the gunman as the avalanche of books fell from the shelves, burying him.

In the silence that followed, Herculeah took off for the dining room. By the time she got to the entrance hall, she was running full out.

She tripped over the gunman's satchel and fell forward. She yelped with surprise.

She scrambled to her feet. Behind her, in the living room were sounds of the gunman struggling to get out from under the books.

She ran through the dining room. Behind her was a sound—a soft pop as if a balloon were exploding. She heard a thud on the bookshelf as she passed—a bullet. He was firing from the floor. He wasn't on his feet yet but he soon would be.

She cut into the kitchen. She remembered the chair she had stumbled over, remembered the fallen books. She couldn't see them but she vaulted over them as if she were a hurdler.

In the living room more books were being thrown

aside. The man was scrambling to his feet. He fell heavily—the boards of the house shook. He got up again.

Now she heard his footsteps. The man was moving fast. He was in the entrance now. Somehow he had survived the books, thrown them off. He had his gun. He had used it and would use it again.

Herculeah reached the back door. Her hands were trembling violently, but she managed to throw the bolt and open the lock.

The man was at the door of the kitchen now. He started forward. He lost his footing on the fallen books, stumbled over the fallen chair, and fell with a curse.

Herculeah hurled herself out the door and slammed it shut behind her. Maybe the gunman would have trouble with the lock, and that would give her a few extra seconds. She knew she needed all the time she could get.

Glass shattered behind her. The gunman was at the door. He was going to fire.

She zigzagged down the alley in short desperate strides. The cat darted out of her way, cringing in fear.

She looked up. She could see Uncle Neiman there, the car parked right at the entrance.

She opened the door and threw herself into the right seat.

"Get out of here," she gasped. "He's coming." She grabbed his arm as if to shake him into action. "Get out of here!"

She glanced back. The gunman was in the alley. "Drive!"

24

Uncle Neiman caught her fear. He tried to turn on the ignition and found it was already on. He released the brake. He threw the car in gear and stepped on the gas in one motion. The car shot forward.

"Turn the corner!"

"Which way?"

"Any way! Left! Left!"

She pointed, glancing back over her shoulder. The gunman was there. He started after them on foot. He stopped and raised his pistol, holding it with both hands.

"Turn! Turn!" she cried.

117

"I—"

Herculeah grabbed the steering wheel and turned it herself. The car made the corner, and Herculeah straightened the wheel. Helplessly, Uncle Neiman tried to regain control of the car, but Herculeah was at the wheel now.

"Faster! Faster!"

"I can't go any faster," he protested. "I can't see."

"Well, I can! I've got the wheel. You just give it some gas. Faster. He's behind us. Faster! Faster!"

They took the next corner with the tires squealing.

"Is he still there?"

"Yes."

"You see him?"

"No, I don't see him, but he's still there. Turn here!"

"I can't."

Herculeah spun the steering wheel around and they made the corner. Herculeah glanced at the street ahead. "Ah," she said. "We're back in traffic."

"Well, don't stop steering."

"Let's get about four or five blocks between us and him and then we'll pull over. I wish I could see a phone booth."

"Did you get it?" Uncle Neiman asked.

"What?"

"The money."

"No! No! How can you think about your stupid money when I was almost—Brakes!"

Uncle Neiman put on the brakes and they both fell forward.

"I can't stop trembling." Herculeah took one hand off the steering wheel to show him. "You probably can't see that, but it's shaking like a leaf."

"I can feel it."

"This is probably far enough. Slow down."

Uncle Neiman slowed and Herculeah steered them into a parking place.

She sighed.

"Where are we?" Uncle Neiman asked.

"I don't know. I don't care. I'm alive. That's all that matters to me."

She leaned her head back against the headrest.

"I'm alive . . . I'm alive . . ."

"So why didn't you get the money?"

"Because he came in. *He* came in. He—"

She broke off, unable to finish. What had happened was too fresh. When she thought of it, it was as if it were happening all over again. She shuddered.

"He is a very, very big man, big as a bull, and—you probably won't believe this—but he has red eyes."

"I believe it," Uncle Neiman said.

She knew she would never forget that terrible moment when their eyes had met—those hooded eyes that seemed to have been lit up by a light of their own.

She put her hands over her eyes to block out the sight. Her knees were trembling. She began to gasp for air. She felt she would never get enough breath into her air-starved lungs.

"Are you all right?" Uncle Neiman asked, peering at her in the dim light.

"I need some air."

She rolled down her window, and he did too, sending fresh air through the front seat and across her face. She felt as if she might have a fever.

"Is that better?"

"I guess so."

He hesitated. He was still peering at her anxiously.

"Yes, that's better."

"Then maybe we better get going."

"Get going?" she asked incredulously. "Where?"

"I don't know." Uncle Neiman only knew he was eager to be back on the road. "That worked good with you steering and me doing the rest."

"It did not work well. We are lucky to be alive. Those were desperate measures for a desperate situation. If we hadn't gotten away from that man—"

She sat up and glanced back over her shoulder, half expecting to see the gunman there, shoving aside pedestrians with those powerful shoulders, running through traffic, turning those terrible red eyes right and left to find them.

"Oh!" she cried.

"What? What is it?"

"Oh!"

"What? Is he here?"

"It's a police car! There's a police car!"

"Where?" Uncle Neiman asked, glancing around blindly. He was in some ways more afraid of the police than he was of the gunman.

He attempted to turn the steering wheel and get them back out in the road, but Herculeah reached over and held on with an iron grip.

She leaned her head out and waved one arm, not letting go of the steering wheel with the other.

Then Herculeah yelled the words she had been wanted to yell all this afternoon, all her life, it seemed.

"Help! Help!"

25
HOME

"There's a car! There's a car!" Meat cried.

He was still at the window. All his mother's pleas had not moved him. His one concession had been to put on his pajamas. Finally his mother had given up and gone upstairs to her bedroom.

Although Meat didn't know it, his mother had not gone to bed either and was standing at the upstairs window, directly above him, watching too.

"Lieutenant Jones is getting out of the car," he announced.

He held his breath. Then he was flooded with such joy that tears came to his eyes.

122

"Mom, it's Herculeah! She's all right! She's back! She's walking up the steps."

He started for the front door.

His mother came down the steps fast enough to stop him. "Albert, you can't go out there."

He glanced out the window beside the door. Across the street, the door was flung open, and Mrs. Jones rushed out to embrace Herculeah. She pulled back to look at Herculeah, to make sure she was really there and all right. Then she hugged her again.

"I've got to go. Mom, they'll be in the house in a minute."

"Exactly where they need to be."

"Mom—" He struggled with her.

"Albert, you're in your pajamas."

"But I've got to know what happened."

"I want to know what happened too, but we cannot disturb them now. That girl has been through a terrible time. Her father had to actually help her up the steps."

Meat peered out the window again. His shoulders sagged with disappointment.

"Now they're in the house," he cried in anguish. "Now it's too late."

"The news about Herculeah will keep until morning, as will the news about poor Neiman. Now go to bed."

"Mom—"

"I agreed you could stay up until you knew about Herculeah. Now you know. Go to bed, Albert."

Suddenly Meat was too tired to argue. He started slowly up the stairs, pulling himself along by the banister.

The phone rang. "I'll get it," he said quickly. He started down the steps.

His mother was quicker. She picked up the phone on the second ring.

Meat came down the three remaining steps and stood beside her. She tilted the phone so he could hear the conversation.

"Mrs. McMannis?"

"Yes."

"This is Chico Jones."

"Yes?"

"I saw your light on, and I knew you were anxious about your brother."

"Oh, yes."

"Your brother is unharmed."

Meat felt the tension go out of her body and the relief flood in.

"Oh, thank you. And your daughter?"

Meat held his breath.

"Herculeah's unharmed as well. She's exhausted and shaky, but her mother's getting her to bed."

"Where is Neiman, Lieutenant Jones?"

"Your brother's in custody now."

"Custody?"

"Partly for his own protection, ma'am. We haven't got the killer yet. We know his identity. He left an arsenal of weapons at the bookshop. His fingerprints were all over everything, but we haven't got him."

"Will there be—" Meat's mother paused, apparently familiar with the right word but unable to say it.

Meat supplied it. "Charges?"

"There may be, but there do seem to be extenuating circumstances. Well, I'm sure you need to get to bed. I'll be staying over here tonight, so if there's any trouble, you give me a call. I'll be standing by."

"Thank you very much, Lieutenant."

She put down the phone.

"What a lovely, thoughtful, kind man," she said.

"I thought you didn't like him. You're always criticizing both Herculeah's parents."

"A person can occasionally be wrong," she said.

26

"They got him!"

Meat said, "Herculeah?"

He was sitting by the kitchen phone waiting until nine o'clock. That was the absolute earliest his mother would allow him to call. But Herculeah beat him to it.

"Yes! It's me! They got him." There was a shocked silence so Herculeah added, "The gunman! They got the gunman!"

Meat was already sitting down, but he felt as if he had just gotten lower with relief.

"Guess where they got him?" she went on.

126

"I can't."

"At Death's Door. He went back for his guns. This man was not terribly bright."

"If he was bright at all," Meat commented, "he wouldn't be a hired killer."

"Too right," Herculeah said. "I was hoping you'd stayed home from school today. Can you come over?"

"If they've got the gunman, I can. Otherwise my mom would make me stay in the house for the rest of my life."

"I'm having a cup of coffee. My dad said I deserved it."

"Is there enough for me?"

"Of course."

"I'm on my way."

When Meat was sitting across from Herculeah, waiting for his coffee to cool he said, "My mom wouldn't let me call. She said you needed your rest."

"Actually, I have been awake since dawn," Herculeah said.

"Didn't your mother let you sleep in?"

"My mother did. Tarot didn't. At first light the parrot started yelling, 'Beware, beware.' I said, 'Go back to sleep. It's too early for that.' But Tarot kept it up. 'Beware. Beware.' Finally my mother came and took him out of the room, but I could hear him all the way down the hall."

"Did your dad explain what happened? I'm still not sure about things."

"I know everything. What happened was that a man named Piranna—it sounds like the fish, but it's spelled differently—"

"A homophone," Meat said.

Herculeah looked at him in surprise. "How did you know that?"

He tried to act as if it were nothing. He took a small sip of coffee and was proud that he swallowed it without spitting it back into the mug. He managed a modest shrug.

"That's what I love about you, Meat—that you come up with things like homophone."

He blushed with pleasure. He would remember that sentence until the day he died—the first part anyway.

"So, this fish guy, this Piranna," she pronounced the word carefully and grinned at him, "he shot at the mayor.

"And your uncle Neiman may not be able to see very well, but like a lot of people with a handicap, his other senses go into overdrive to make up for it. So Uncle Neiman has great hearing.

"In fact he was the only one who heard the shot. He looked up—right at the window where it came from—but he couldn't see a thing.

"The gunman—piranha Piranna"—she grinned at

Meat again—"panicked. He had to get out of town, but first he hired a gunman to take care of Uncle Neiman. Uncle Neiman's newspaper picture was still in the gunman's duffel bag."

"Where is Uncle Neiman now—still in custody?"

"No. He's back in his apartment over the shop."

"That's a relief."

"And guess what they called the gunman?"

"I couldn't."

"They called him the Bull."

She gave a slight shudder, remembering how well the name had fit. In her nightmare she still saw those terrifying red eyes.

"Bull?"

"Yes, don't you get it? The Cretan Bull! You're the one who told me about it when I had my last premonition. Capturing it was one of the labors of Hercules."

Meat said nothing.

"Isn't it exciting?"

"What?"

"I'm following almost exactly in the footsteps of Hercules."

27
TICKLED TO DEATH

"So this is the famous hat?"

It was a woman's voice. She was speaking from the entrance to Death's Door.

Both Herculeah and Meat looked up from their work. Meat waited a moment. When no one answered, he called out, "Yes, it is."

"Oh, there you are." The woman glanced into the room, waved at them and went back to the hat.

Uncle Neiman had put his hat under a large glass dome. It stood on a table beside the cash register and had become sort of a tourist attraction. The woman admired it a moment more.

"And there's the bullet hole," she said almost reverently.

Neither Meat nor Herculeah answered, though Meat unconsciously rubbed the side of his head as if to assure himself there was no hole there. The woman crossed to where they were working.

"And are you the person who was wearing that hat when it got that bullet hole?"

Meat nodded.

"And you're the girl who almost got shot, too?"

"I sure am."

"Well, now I've seen all the celebrities but the one I came to see. Magoo, where are you?"

"In the rentals," he called back.

The woman disappeared through the doorway, and Herculeah and Meat went back to sorting books. Both shelves—this one and the one Herculeah had pushed over on top of the gunman—were now erect. Herculeah and Meat were reshelving the books.

They were working on the Gs. Meat was taking great satisfaction in his work. "Gillis . . . Gilman . . . George, Elizabeth, goes back there. Grafton—she belongs in the Gr's. You're doing those, aren't you?"

He held out the book to her. She didn't take it. He looked around. She didn't even seem to see it. "Here!" he said.

"Oh."

Herculeah took the book in a distracted way and set it on an empty shelf. Meat was suddenly aware that Herculeah had stopped working altogether.

She was holding one book in her hands. She was not staring at it, but looking into the distance.

"Did you find something interesting?"

Herculeah nodded.

Still she didn't look at him or the book in her hands.

"Uncle Neiman will give you any book you want to read—me too. He says the shop is ours."

"I don't want to read it."

"What is it?"

She turned the book over in her lap so that the title was hidden.

"So? What's the big secret?"

"It's not a big secret. I just picked up this book, and I had a premonition about something."

"Your premonitions usually work," Meat said uneasily. "I didn't believe your last one about the bull, but it turned out to be true."

Herculeah didn't say anything.

"So what's the premonition?"

Herculeah glanced up as if to check the books she'd shelved. "Not yet." She dropped the book in her lap, picked up two others from a pile and shelved one.

"Anyway I never had a premonition your uncle was going to kidnap me."

Meat glanced at the door. "You know he doesn't like that word."

"Well, he better get used to it. I've had to get used to some hard things, too. It was not easy for me to come back here to Death's Door, the very spot where I was almost killed."

"Yes, but you're stronger than most everybody. You could do something like that. Uncle Neiman is more like me." He was going to add the word "unhardy," but he decided not to.

Herculeah shrugged.

"So what's the title of the book?"

She didn't answer. She glanced down in her lap. She seemed to be in a world of her own. Meat hated it when she shut him out like that.

"At least tell me the author, If I knew the author, then I could find one of her books. They'd have her other titles inside."

When she didn't answer, he said, "Well it has to start with G."

"No, H. It was out of place." She smiled, as if at herself. "The reason I'm not telling you is that this makes no sense at all."

"Let me be the judge of that."

She hesitated, then turned the book around so he could see the title.

"*Funny Bones.*" He read the words aloud. "You're right. It makes no sense."

"I told you. All the same, Meat, when I picked this book up, I got a premonition."

"I do not think one of Hercules' labors had anything to do with bones. And they certainly weren't funny."

"I know. Maybe I'm safe at last."

Herculeah put the book on the shelf. She watched it for a moment and then smiled at Meat.

Meat didn't smile back. He had a premonition of his own.

"I wouldn't count on it," he said.